The Best Sex I Ever Had

*Adult Stories Written by Real Men
Recounting Their Hottest Sexual
Encounters, Featuring Rough, Anal, BDSM,
Gangbangs, Domination, Threesomes, and
Older-Younger Daddy Erotica*

Rayna Russell

Contents

Introduction

The biggest surprise I've had as an editor of adult fiction is how active this community of readers is. So many of you have taken the time to reach out and tell me what you like (… and what you don't like) in the short story collections I've published so far. I love hearing from you!

Reach out anytime:

RaynaRussellErotica@gmail.com

One thing that you have told me, dear readers, is how much you like writers who are men, with their particular point of view when it comes to erotic writing. Another thing you enjoy, you naughty readers, is when the stories are based on real events, not some imagined fantasy.

With those two criteria in mind, I bring you "The Best Sex I Ever Had."

I reached out to my favorite male writers and simply asked them to tell me about the best sex they ever had. And what they sent me... is nothing short of amazing.

Fun fact: Many of them chose pen names this time because these are stories they've never told before, and they don't want to get a reputation!

These stories are all real. They're all written by real men. And my writers do NOT hold back.

Sit back. Relax. And enjoy.

With love and admiration,

Rayna

Chapter 1

Dave

By Dave Waringer

I liked machines.

I understood them, and they spoke to me in a way that nothing else did. Each morning, when I woke up, the first thing I did was reach for my glasses. Then I scrolled through my phone to read the latest in high-tech news. At night, I came home to an empty apartment and skimmed through the shows being offered, all of them sci-fi shows I'd seen before.

I didn't keep up with sports, and I had no idea how they were played.

Everything in my life had been the same until a few days before my thirtieth birthday when my girlfriend of a few months showed up at my apartment. After a long and winding conversation, she ended up breaking up with me and walked out the door. Yet, it didn't surprise me one bit.

Hell, it didn't even bother me.

Claire was just the latest in a long list of girlfriends who didn't satisfy me.

Not in the way I wanted to be satisfied.

Days later, when I turned thirty, I made a promise to myself.

In the morning, I got out and maxed out my credit cards buying new expensive clothes for myself. When I finished, I went to the barber for a new, edgier haircut and walked out with a newfound confidence and a spring in my step. In another store, I was tempted to break my glasses, but the shop woman stopped me.

She handed me a brand-new pair of contacts and another pair for free.

I checked out the perky blonde-haired shop attendant who helped me put them in, and I kept coming up with excuses to touch her. As soon as she was done, she pulled back and smiled at me. That night, I found myself on the phone with a personal trainer who agreed to help me get a membership to the gym a few blocks away and take me on as a client. A few weeks later, I was on a business trip I'd aggressively campaigned for, taking out anything and anyone who got in my way.

I was leaning against the bar, my head pounding after a day of being cooped up in a Los Angeles conference room, listening to one pitch after the next, when I saw her. She had sleek chestnut brown hair, heels that clicked against the hardwood floors, and a black dress that hugged her body in all the right places. Even underneath florescent lightning, I could see how beautiful she was.

Every man in the room was gawking at her, except for me.

I didn't want to be like everyone else.

With my new look, she would be the one to come to me, not the other way around.

She gave her hips a little extra sway but fixed her gaze straight ahead, on nothing in particular. Once she reached the bar, she set her purse down and tossed her hair over her shoulders. Her blood-red lips lifted into a half-smile as she gestured to the bartender. He set a dirty martini down in front of her and ambled away.

She took a few sips of her drink. "It's rude to stare, you know."

I stood up straighter and smiled. "It's hard not to when you walk in dressed like that."

Slowly, she twisted to face me, the smile on her face growing wider. "It's a good thing I came over to talk to you then."

Something low and pleasant unfurled in the center of my stomach. "Is that so?"

She placed a hand on my arm, showing off her manicured nails. "Absolutely. I like a strong and confident man who knows what he wants."

I took a long sip of my scotch, and it burned a path down my throat. "And what makes you think I'm that kind of man?"

She made a sweeping hand gesture. "The way you hold yourself. The way you're dressed."

It was finally working.

All the months of hard work and rigid discipline had led me to this moment, sitting across from a gorgeous woman at an LA hotel bar. In the background, laughter rose and fell, punctuated by the sound of music playing through the overhead speakers. Smirking, I leaned forward and held myself still, letting her catch a whiff of my cologne.

"I'm a big fan, too. A really big fan."

She straightened her back and held her hand out. "I'm Jenny."

I took her hand in mine and held her gaze. "Dave."

After a long pause, she withdrew her hand. "So, Dave, what do you do?"

I paused. "I'm a computer programmer."

She leaned against the counter, offering me an ample view of her cleavage. "Do you like your job, Dave?"

I gestured for another drink, but my eyes didn't leave her chest. "I do. How about you? What do you do?"

"You mean when I'm not doing men like you? I'm in marketing." She eyed me over the rim of her glass and lowered her gaze. "It pays the bills."

I curled my fingers around my glass and glanced up. "Good."

Jenny shifted closer, and I caught a scent of her perfume, something floral that sent a jolt to my stomach. "What do you say we keep this party going?"

I took a long sip of my drink and ignored the dip in my stomach. "What did you have in mind?"

"We can go back upstairs to my room." Jenny kept leaning forward until her mouth was pressed to my ear, and I was glancing down at the low cut of her dress and staring at the swell of her breasts. "A man like you looks like he can fuck me hard—just the way I like."

The pounding in my skull was replaced with something else—something that burned and scorched. Jenny took my lobe between her teeth and tugged, sending a jolt of nervousness through me. When I placed a hand on her hips and buried my face in the crook of her neck, she melted against me.

It was finally happening, but I didn't want her to sense how nervous I was.

My stomach was twisted into tight knots as I drew back and reached into my pocket. After paying for our drinks, I kept my hand on her waist and steered her in the direction of the elevator. It slid open, and we got on at the same time. When it pinged shut and no one else joined us, I pushed her against the wall.

She gave me a breathless smile and lowered the straps of her dress. "How do you want me?"

"Wrap your legs around me," I instructed in a thick voice. "And don't move unless I tell you to."

Jenny's lips parted, and she nodded. Her hazel eyes stayed on me as she hoisted herself up and wrapped her legs around my torso. Then she lowered the straps of her dress further, revealing the black lacy bra underneath. I ignored the tremor racing through me as I rubbed myself against her. She made a low whimpering sound when I placed a hand on her chest.

I squeezed her breasts hard.

She threw her head back and dug her nails into my back. "That feels so good."

I cupped the back of her neck and tilted it up. "You know what would feel even better? I can't wait to have you on all fours."

Being with a woman like that was already working its charm.

I was going to have her begging for me before the night was over.

Jenny whimpered again, and it reverberated inside of my head.

I captured her lips with mine and thrust against the lower half of her body. Her hands moved from the back of my neck to my shoulders. Then her fingers ducked underneath my button-down shirt and glided over my skin. She tasted like sweet red wine and peppermint. I used my tongue to explore every inch of her mouth until the blood was roaring in my ears.

Jenny and I bucked against each other, slowly at first, then faster and faster.

She was pawing at my back and panting when the elevator doors pinged open. A younger couple stood there in shock, and I gave the woman a slow and lazy smile as I turned around. Her face was hot as she watched me set Jenny down on her feet and give her ass a firm slap. Then I lined up behind her and draped an arm over her waist. I angled my other arm so it covered her exposed chest, feeling the nipples press against my skin. Jenny said nothing as we walked down the empty, carpeted hallway. In the doorway to her room, she stopped and reached into her purse. I glanced over my shoulders at the woman gawking at us, her chest heaving unevenly.

Yes, that's it. I'm coming for you next, baby.

With a sigh, I released Jenny, and while she fumbled with the door, I ran my hands over her back. Stopping at her ass, I gave it a firm squeeze and rubbed myself against it. My erection was already straining against my pants, and I knew something needed to be done. Half of me was tempted to beckon the red-haired woman over for some more fun. But her boyfriend led her onto the elevator, and I switched my attention back to Jenny. The door clicked open, and Jenny leaned back into my touch, and I could smell her.

I could smell how much she wanted me.

"Should we go inside?"

I pushed her hair forward and kissed the back of her neck. "Or we could stay out here, and I could fuck you in the hallway where everyone can see."

God knew they could all use a nice little show, and I'm sure the men would appreciate Jenny's tits bouncing up and down.

Jenny's hand moved to the back of my neck. "I want you."

I placed her arms on either side of the wall and positioned myself directly behind her so she could feel me through my pants. "How much do you want me?"

Jenny released a deep, shaky breath. "You can fuck me right here. As long as you fuck me good."

I smiled and sank my teeth into her neck.

She gripped the back of my head, and my hands went to her breasts. She was heaving now, and it took everything in me not to bend her over right then and there. While a part of me relished the thought of having her completely at my mercy, especially in the hallway of a hotel like this, another part of me knew I had to reign it in.

Jenny and I had big plans, and I had no intention of ruining them by getting kicked out.

Abruptly, I stopped rubbing myself against her and nudged her into the room. "Inside. Right now."

Inside, it was dark except for a small lamp on the table next to the couch, casting long shadows across the walls. I kicked the door shut with the back of my leg, and my hands went to the buttons of my shirt. I undid one after the other in quick succession until it fell to the floor with a flutter. Jenny was standing a few feet away, her pupils dilated and her chest still rising and falling unevenly.

"Take off your clothes," I instructed in a low voice. "I want a show."

She nodded, and her hands went to the hem of her dress. Slowly, she wriggled her hips and pulled it over her head, revealing a smooth and tanned body and a belly button piercing that glistened in the pale light of the moon. When she was done, she tossed her dress into a heap on the floor and spun around, so I could see her back.

And the butterfly tattoo stamped on her lower back.

Damn, I really had hit the jackpot.

Wordlessly, Jenny bent down so her ass was hanging in the air. She hooked her fingers through her black lace underwear and pulled it down. When she stepped out of it, I curled my hands into fists and admired the way her pussy glistened. Then her hands went to the clasp of her bra, and she undid it, allowing her breasts to spill forward. I hurried out of my pants and left my boxers on.

"Come here and undress me."

Jenny spun around to face me, her heels clicking with every move. She pulled my boxers down with her teeth, and when she was on her knees, she stopped. I kicked them away and gripped the back of her neck. In one quick move, I pulled her up and crushed my mouth against hers. She moaned and whimpered as my hands moved down to her waist, and I hoisted her up. She locked her legs around my waist as I carried her to the bed.

We fell down, and I rubbed my hands up and down her arms.

Her skin broke out into goosebumps as I moved against her.

She raked her fingers over my back, sending dual waves of pain and pleasure through me. I dropped a hand between us and stroked her. She bucked and arched her back. I pushed one finger in, then another, marveling at how wet she was. Using my free hand, I rolled her nipples between my fingers. She was sweating and panting my name when I stopped moving my fingers inside of her. Without warning, I sat back on my legs and watched her.

Jenny stared at me through hooded eyes. "What happened?"

"Touch yourself," I said in a voice I didn't recognize. "I want you to touch yourself. Imagine I'm the one who's touching you."

Bitch was going to make me come too soon with the way she was moaning and moving.

And I couldn't have that.

Jenny shoved her hair out of her eyes and lowered herself onto the mattress. She spread her legs open, a hand sliding down between her thighs. Her other hand pressed her breasts together. She looked directly at me as she pushed one finger in, then another. I let one hand fall to my side, and the other ran over the length of my shaft.

Fuck.

This wasn't Jenny's first time, but I didn't want her to think it was mine.

I wanted her begging for me and unable to move for hours.

I wanted her to remember this night forever.

I wanted to ensure no man would ever satisfy her like I would.

Rather than bury myself in her like I was desperate to, I let her continue to pleasure herself. When she was close, I took both of her hands in mine and lifted them over her head. She squirmed when I positioned myself at her entrance and held myself still. Her face was covered in sweat as she squirmed and tried to link her fingers over my torso, pulling me closer. Using one hand, I kept her arms in a vicelike grip, and, using the other, I gave her feet a light slap.

"Not until I say so," I whispered. I nipped on her bottom lip and thrust into her. Jenny cried out when I eased out and slammed back in. Then, I secured her feet around my torso. She panted and bucked against me, but I wouldn't release her hands.

It felt good to be the one calling the shots.

And all I needed to give her was one flick, one word, and she was mine.

The bed dipped and creaked as I rammed in and out of her, letting the smell and feel of her wash over me. Jenny's breath quickened as her release came. Her body writhed and spasmed under me, shaking violently the whole time. I stopped thrusting and glanced down at her. Her mouth was parted, and she was licking her lips.

"Why did you stop?"

I eased out of her and helped her sit up. "On all fours. Now."

Jenny sat up and gave me another sultry look. She turned around, braced herself on her elbows, and spared me a look over her shoulders. "Like this?"

I stroked her ass and rubbed myself against her. "That's a good little girl. You like being bad, don't you, Jenny?"

She groaned. "I do."

I gripped her hips with both hands and positioned myself at her entrance. "Tell me more."

Jenny swung her gaze back to the front and exhaled. "I...oh, that feels good."

I reached between us and played with her nipples. "If you want me to keep fucking you, you're going to have to tell me more."

Jenny wriggled her hips and blew out another breath. "I want you."

I thrust into her and circled my hips. "You want me to what?"

"I want you to fuck me," Jenny groaned, each word punctuated with a moan. "Please, Dave. *Please.*"

I slammed into her, filling her to the hilt. "I like the sound of you begging."

I pinned one arm behind her back, and Jenny fell face forward into the pillow. With slow and precise movements, I eased in and out of her until she was crying out my name again and again. I pinched her ass, her nipples, and everything else I could. She kept crying out for more, for me to take her harder, and I squeezed my eyes shut.

Jenny came again, even harder than before, and her muscles clenched.

I waited until she was no longer heaving to ease out of her. She spun around to face me as I stood up. I cocked a finger in her direction, and she crawled over to the edge of the bed. She was on her hands and knees, at eye level with my bulging cock.

It was the hottest thing I had ever seen.

Her cum was still all over me as I rubbed myself against her mouth. "Open up like a good little girl."

Jenny smiled and braced herself on her elbows. Using her tongue, she licked a path down my sides and then back up to my shaft. When she took me into her mouth, my vision went white. I gripped the back of her neck and pumped into her. I started off slowly, wanting to drag this on for as long as possible. But when she sunk her nails into my waist and squeezed her eyes shut, something else took over.

I thrust in and out of her mouth with wild and animal-like abandon.

I felt invincible and powerful, like nothing in the world could possibly stop me.

She made low gagging sounds when I gripped the back of her neck and held her still. I glanced down at her face and saw the thin sheen of sweat on her forehead. Then I reached between us and flicked her nipples. A jolt coursed through her as she lifted her gaze to mine, and I saw the desire there.

Abruptly, I yanked her head back and waited till she looked up at me. "Do you want me to keep mouth fucking you?"

Jenny licked her lips. "Yes."

"Take my cock all the way. And don't stop," I said, my heart hammering louder now. "Don't stop until I come all over your face."

Jenny lowered her gaze and nodded. "Yes, sir."

I fucked her like my life depended on it, like her life did, too. I thrust the way I'd seen men do in porn, hard and without stopping. My inner alpha was reeling in victory and goading me to do more as I climbed onto the bed, and Jenny fell backward. I braced myself against the headboard as I pumped in and out of her mouth.

Eventually, a violent tremor coursed through me as I wrenched myself out of her mouth.

I came all over her face, spraying her with my powerful seed as she lay there, smiling up at me. Once I was done, she licked her lips again.

Then she smiled and sat up straighter. "You're the hottest man I've ever met."

Chapter 2

Ken

by Ken Cooper

Opening up a sports bar was the best goddamn decision I'd ever made.

Second only to leaving my shrill and ungrateful wife.

Thank God she'd gotten sick of me first, so I didn't have to pay her anything extra.

Stupid, sexless bitch.

As I sat in my office in the back, watching the crowd through a thin veil of smoke, I couldn't help but sneak glances at Vanessa. She was in her short red skirt, with a white shirt tucked underneath her. Each time she bent over, she tossed her blonde hair over her shoulders, and I imagined winding my fingers through it. I saw myself gripping the back of her neck as I pumped in and out of her ass.

Fuck me.

I'd been thinking about Vanessa ever since she'd walked into my bar a few months ago and demanded a job. With her full pouty lips, a rack that everyone for miles on end admired, and an ass that was the object of more than their fair share of wet fantasies, including mine, Vanessa had me in the palm of her hands. Although she was twenty-one and only there to work her way through college, she had proven herself to be indispensable.

She was the first to show up in the morning, and the last one to clock out.

She wiped down tables, took orders, and made drinks all with the same kind of precision, and the same suggestive smile on her face. Since I hired her, more and more male customers have been coming in, fighting to be seated in her section. She handled all the attention well and never once let it affect her work.

Even when the male customers tried to get a little handsy, she was able to find a way to put them in their place without it turning into a scene. She handled the attention like a pro, and it only made me wonder more about her.

That girl really was going places, and as I continued to watch her through my thin veil of smoke, I wondered why she'd chosen to work at a sports bar. A young and attractive woman like herself had a future, the kind that most people dreamed about, and I couldn't figure out why she'd chosen my bar of all places. Even if I was grateful each time she bent over to pick something up, or whenever she leaned over the bar to get something. That night, a few more of the waitresses came in, all of them young and with a thirst to prove themselves.

More and more customers flocked in their wake.

Having young, smoking hot waitresses was a lot more beneficial than I had thought it would be.

I was smiling to myself and swirling my whiskey around when Vanessa stepped behind the bar. She glanced over her shoulders and looked directly at me. I sat up straighter behind my desk and tilted the glass in her direction. She smiled as her green eyes bore into mine. Abruptly, I broke our gaze and returned my attention to the stack of paperwork on my desk.

Keep it in your pants; otherwise, it's going to cost you.

Vanessa was hot, and I'd imagined her banging body on several occasions, but I wasn't stupid enough to shit where I ate.

For hours, I half-listened to the music from behind my closed door while I went over the numbers. When I was done, I stood up and stretched. Then I walked over to the window that peered onto the half-lit street and the park across the way. Out of the corner of my eye, I saw a flash of movement, and a half-dressed couple raced past.

The two of them stopped in front of the wrought-iron gates of the park and started to kiss.

The boy pushed the girl up against the wall and began to fondle her. Even from where I stood, I could see how much she was enjoying it, how much more of him she wanted. He rubbed himself against her, and her head fell forward. I eyed them over the rim of my glass and ignored the tightening of my stomach.

I needed to stop imagining myself fucking Vanessa.

Jesus.

She was one of the best waitresses I had and extremely popular with our patrons. Any night she came into work she ended up raking in tips, and I wasn't going to risk all that because my throbbing cock had other ideas. With a frown, I finished the rest of my drink and went back to my desk.

Fucking focus, Ken. She's half your age and probably doesn't want anything to do with your shriveled-up old ass. A girl like that probably has a boyfriend who eats her out every morning or something. Probably likes her to blow him every night, too.

Sometime later, I got up to pour myself another drink. The clock on the wall read two in the morning as I pushed my office door open. With everyone else gone for the night, the bar was unusually quiet and smelled like lemon-scented air freshener. I stepped into the kitchen and rooted through the fridge. When I heard a pair of footsteps round the corner, I spun around and did a double take. Vanessa's curly hair framed her heart-shaped face, and her shirt was untucked but clung to her skin.

"What are you still doing here? It's late." I took a container of food out of the fridge and kicked it shut. "Don't you have to go home and study?"

Vanessa tucked her hair behind her ears. "I wanted to talk to you about something, Mr. Marsters—"

I brushed past her and went back into the office. There, I lit up a cigar and twisted to face her. "You know I hate to be called that. What can I do for you, Vanessa?"

Vanessa shifted from one foot to the other. "I got into a full-time college out of state, so I'll be leaving soon."

I smiled and stared at her through the smoke. "I knew you were meant for bigger things."

Vanessa blinked. "You did?"

I blew out a ring of smoke. "Absolutely. You're meant for a lot more than this sports bar."

Vanessa stepped forward, and her tongue darted out to lick her lips. "Before I go, I wanted to tell you how much I've enjoyed working here."

I smiled and nodded. "Good."

"No, I mean I've loved working here for you. I loved coming here a few times a week and knowing you were going to be around, watching me."

I raised an eyebrow, and my cock perked at the words. "Is that so?"

What game was she playing? And why was she looking at me through lowered lashes?

Vanessa nodded. "I've had a crush on you since I first saw you. You know what I've always wanted to call you?"

I shook my head.

"Daddy," Vanessa whispered, her eyes never leaving my face. "You're the hottest man I've ever seen."

I blew another puff of smoke in her face. "You had anything to drink tonight?"

Vanessa shook her head and licked her lips again. "Absolutely not. I'm stone-cold sober, boss."

No one had ever called me Daddy before, but I liked it. I liked the way it sounded falling from her lips and the way she was looking at me like she wanted to be screwed, relentlessly. Wordlessly, I tossed my cigar into an ashtray, and my hands went to my belt. Vanessa covered the distance between us and kissed me. She removed my belt in one quick move and pulled down my pants and boxer shorts. I cupped the back of her neck and kissed her back, tasting her cherry-flavored lip gloss and bubble gum.

I felt every inch of her body through her thin clothes.

Vanessa rubbed herself against me, and I could feel her nipples poking me through her shirt. With a smirk, I dropped one hand between us and flicked them. She made a little whimpering sound and draped herself over me. I shifted so the back of my knees were pressed against the desk.

Vanessa was kissing me like she was some rabid animal.

Damn, I knew she had a wild streak.

Already, I could tell it was going to take more than one round to satisfy her, and I was rock hard at the thought of her soaking wet pussy.

I massaged the back of her head and explored her mouth. Her tongue darted out, and we began a sensual battle for dominance.

For a twenty-one-year-old, she sure knew how to kiss.

I wondered what else she could do with that skilled mouth of hers.

And how she would feel wrapped around my dick.

With a smile, Vanessa dropped a hand between us and began to stroke me. She moved slowly at first, running her fingers steadily up and down my shaft. My ears were roaring when she rubbed herself against me, and I growled. I wrenched my lips away and attacked her neck with hot, open-mouthed kisses. Vanessa didn't release her grip on me. When I was fully erect, she stopped pumping me and got on her hands and knees.

She placed one hand on my waist, and the other stroked my balls. "God, you're so big."

I grabbed the back of her neck and squeezed. "You haven't seen anything yet."

Vanessa blew out a breath. "I can't wait to taste you, Daddy."

With that, she curled her lips around my shaft. She ran her tongue along the edge, slowly, as if she had all the time in the world. I glanced down at the top of her head, and my pulse quickened. She sucked and licked until she took all of me into her mouth. I eased in and out of her, enjoying how it felt to have her hot and willing mouth wrapped around my throbbing cock.

It was better than anything I could've imagined.

I liked Vanessa on her knees in front of me, her hair a wild mess around her face.

I liked her full pouty lips pleasuring me like I was the only man in the world.

And when I dropped a hand between us to press her breasts together, I liked how her body reacted, her nipples growing hard at my touch.

With a growl, I tugged on the edge of her shirt, and Vanessa stopped sucking on me. She stood up to pull off her shirt, and her skirt followed, leaving her lacy red underwear, and a matching bra.

Fuck me.

I was riveted as she got down on her knees again and braced her hands on either side of her. Her tongue was wicked and wild, and it moved in all sorts of ways. In a way I hadn't experienced in years. She dug her nails into my waist, and I gripped the back of her neck harder. I thrust in and out of her slowly, in practiced strokes, then faster and faster until she was choking. Her eyes were wide and full of hunger as she took me in.

Abruptly, I stopped and pulled her up to her knees. "Let's go. I want to be balls deep in you."

Vanessa smiled and unhooked her bra. "Whatever you want, Daddy."

I took her to into the bar where the counter was, and she hoisted herself up. Using two fingers, she pulled her panties down and over her ankles. When she threw them away, she cocked a finger at me, and I stepped in between her legs. I wasted no time thrusting into her and groaning. She linked her feet around my waist and raked her fingers over my back.

"Fuck. You're so tight."

Vanessa brought her lips next to my ear. "Only for you, Daddy."

"That's right." I braced my hands on either side of the counter and eased in and out of her. "Only I can make you this wet. Do you understand me?"

"Only you can make me this wet and this horny." Vanessa took my lobe between her teeth and tugged. "Yes, that's it. Fuck me harder."

I dropped my head to take one nipple between my teeth. "I knew you'd taste good. I fucking knew it."

She threw her head back and met each thrust with a buck of her own. "Don't stop."

I moved to the other nipple and tugged and bit until they were both as hard as pebbles. Vanessa continued to rake her fingernails over my back, marking me as hers. I lifted her legs over my shoulders and rammed into her. She was so wet I could smell every last inch of her, and all I could think about was how much more I wanted.

I wanted every last part of her supple and taut body.

I wanted her under me and over me, with her breasts bouncing up and down. And I wanted to be buried so far inside of her that neither of us could walk.

Vanessa's breath quickened as she dug her nails into my shoulders. She draped her back over the bar and pressed her breasts together. Her release was quick, and it made her whole body shake. As soon as she came down from her high, she shifted and moved away. I watched her as she climbed onto the counter and glanced at me over her shoulders.

Vanessa bit down on her bottom lip. "What else do you want to do to me, Daddy? Do you want to fuck me from behind?"

I positioned myself at her entrance and thrust. "Have you been a good girl for Daddy?"

Vanessa shook her head. "No, I've been a very bad girl, and I need you to punish me."

I eased out of her and rubbed myself against her. "Like this?"

Vanessa choked out a moan and faced the front again. I gripped her hips with both hands and thrust into her. She ground against me, and the blood continued to roar in my ears. I still couldn't believe she was naked on all fours on the bar counter, letting me bang her brains out.

As if we were both chasing some kind of high.

I sunk nails into her waist and thrust harder, wanting to claim her with every move, every touch, and every grunt. Vanessa's moans were like music to my ears, and I didn't even care that the neighbors could probably hear us by now or that anyone passing by would only have to peer in through the glass window to see us going at it.

The thought of anyone else walking in on us only made it more exciting.

I pressed my head against her back and smiled at the goosebumps that broke out across her skin. "Are you enjoying yourself?"

Vanessa nodded.

I slapped her ass, hard enough to leave a red-shaped mark. "You're going to need to learn to articulate for your Daddy."

"You're so big." Vanessa's voice was hoarse when she spoke, and it sent another wave of desire racing through me. "You really know how to fuck, don't you?"

I squeezed her ass and smirked. "You've never had it this good, have you, princess?"

"Never," Vanessa choked out, her movements growing wilder and more erratic. "They were boys. Nothing compared to you, Daddy."

I reached between us to twist her nipples. "And you're nothing like my wife. She was always so tame in bed, so meek. But you...you like it rough, don't you? You like being dirty."

And I loved that she had chosen me to experience this.

Fucking hell.

I was going to come all over the bar if she didn't stop making those noises. Abruptly, I stopped thrusting and spun her around. Vanessa spread her legs apart and stared at me through hooded eyes. I was sweating and unable to think clearly. Since she was still so wet, I was able to thrust back into her and grip the soles of her feet.

Vanessa lifted her hips off the counter. "Yes, that's it."

I threw her legs over my shoulders and inched in further, so I was all the way to the hilt. As soon as I was, I eased out of her and slammed back again. I did this for a while until Vanessa was writhing and panting and crying my name out like it was some kind of prayer. I squeezed my eyes shut, buried my face in her neck, and sank my teeth there. She clawed at my back, drawing me closer and closer.

With a growl, I deepened the bite, drawing blood between my teeth.

Vanessa didn't flinch or falter.

She linked her feet over my torso and drew me closer. I braced my arms on either side of the bar and used every ounce of self-control I had to hold back. I wanted this to last for hours because there were still so many surfaces, I wanted to take her on. I wanted her in my office, in my chair, on the kitchen counters, over every single booth in the bar.

I wanted her smell and the taste of her on every inch of my skin.

At night, when she goes home, I want my smell to linger on her skin, forcing her to remember what we did to each other. Vanessa threw her head back and cried out, her entire body writhing and spasming as she came. Sweat broke out across her forehead and down the sides of her body. She shook so violently that she rose a little off the counter. Then she slumped back, heaving and pressing a hand to her chest.

Her eyes flew open to look directly at me, and she pressed her breasts together. "How do you want me?"

"Keep touching yourself," I said, in a thick voice. She kept one hand on her breast, and the other glided down over her slick skin and paused at her center. After licking her finger, she pushed it in between her wet folds. Then she added another, and her lips lifted into a sultry smile. I drew back to look at her, pumping steadily the whole time.

Vanessa was a seductress, the kind of woman who knew exactly what she wanted.

She was touching herself in a way that was driving me crazy, it was making me move like I was possessed. It almost felt like I was going to ram us both through the counter which creaked and dipped with each movement. Slowly, Vanessa lifted her head and licked a path from my neck to my ears. When she took my bottom lobe between her lips, I stiffened.

Then she placed both hands on my chest and shoved me.

I staggered back, my mouth half-open. Vanessa took my hand and led me into the office. She pushed me onto the carpet and straddled me in reverse, so her ass was in my face. My heart was pounding loudly as I gripped her hips and sank my mouth in between her wet folds.

She took me into her mouth and moaned.

My entire body shook and jerked as she bucked against me, coaxing my release out of me. When I was done, I collapsed onto the carpet, and Vanessa held me to her. A short while later, she got up and pulled my shirt on. In the kitchen, I found her making food. The omelet pan burned while I fucked her against the refrigerator door, with her hands twisted behind her back.

A few months later, when Vanessa came by for a visit, I took her into my office and placed a hand over her mouth. While customers came in and out of the bar, I fucked her against the wooden door, watching her eyes the entire time. During Christmas, when she came back wearing a large black coat with thigh-high boots and a sexy Santa costume underneath, we ended up fucking in one of the back booths until we both collapsed exhausted and spent and ate half-naked by the fire in my office.

But nothing compared to the first night she came into my office and called me Daddy.

Chapter 3

Ricky

by Ricky Ruiz

"Alright, boys. Let's hustle." I placed one hand in my pockets and watched the group of teenage boys running around the gym, faces shiny with sweat, and a look of fierce concentration etched onto their faces. All of them wore their red and white gym uniform, their shoes squeaking against the hardwood floors.

I stared down at the clipboard and then back up at the team.

Considering how many gym teachers they had gone through in the past few years, they weren't looking half-bad, but I knew they needed something a little more. I'd only been working here for a few weeks, but I wanted to prove myself.

To show my former school that they'd made the right decision in choosing me as their gym teacher.

So, I was keeping the kids after school for an extra hour.

I needed them in tip-top shape if they were going to be ready for the game in a few weeks. With a frown, I lowered the clipboard again and studied them as they ran from one end of the gymnasium to the next, passing the orange ball around. When one of them got hit in the face and a burst of red blood erupted, I blew my whistle and beckoned them forward. Huddled together in a circle, I could see how exhausted they were.

And how much they reeked.

"You were better today, but we still have a lot of work ahead of us. Now, why don't you all hit the showers, and we'll try again the day after tomorrow?"

I glanced around at each of their sweaty and tired faces and then straightened my back. "Go, team."

One by one they began to disperse, but a few of them lingered when the double doors to the gym burst open, and *she* walked in. Kate Fontana, my former English teacher, sauntered in wearing three-inch heels that clicked steadily, a skirt that swished with each movement, and a button-down shirt that left the first few buttons undone.

Some of the boys were openly gawking at her, but she didn't notice.

I was sure she was used to getting that kind of attention with a body like that.

She was still heading directly for me, a small smile painted on her blood-red lips. I shifted from one foot to the other and tried to ignore the racing of my heart. Even after three years away, I still thought of her as the hottest woman I'd ever laid eyes on. And when she came close enough for me to smell her exotic perfume, I suddenly remembered why all of my high school wet dreams starred her.

As a teenager, I'd spent countless nights imagining her in my bed, running her manicured fingers all over me and wrapping her full and luscious lips over my cock. I'd even pleasured myself to thoughts of her, and how it would feel for me to bury myself in her. High school was torture, especially when I had to be in close proximity to her and not able to do anything about it. All through college I thought of her, and I imagined her face and her body whenever I fucked another woman.

After all of this time, she and I were finally on equal footing.

The knowledge sent a quiet thrill through me especially when she stopped in front of me and placed a hand on my arm. "I'm sorry to disturb you, Coach Morales, but I'm going to need some of your team to stay with me after school the day after tomorrow."

I glanced down at her hand and then back up at her face. "We have a game in a few weeks."

Ms. Fontana smiled. "And some of them missed their schoolwork. Jack and Miles especially. I think you and I can agree that schoolwork is important, too."

"Of course, Ms. Fontana, but—"

She inched closer, and when she put a hand on my arm, my stomach tightened. "It's Kate."

I blinked. "Huh?"

"We work together now." Her hand was still on my arm, and she was close enough for me to see the beads of sweat that rolled down her neck and disappeared under her shirt. "I'm not your English teacher anymore, Ricky."

How did my name sound so dirty rolling off her lips?

I cleared my throat and felt something stir in my pants. "Right, well, I'm sure we can come to some sort of agreement."

Kate's smile grew wider. "Good. I'm glad we had this chat."

All too quickly, she withdrew her hand and took a step back. "You should stop by later."

I paused. "Stop by?"

"Happy hour for new teachers at O'Malley's," Kate replied after a brief pause. "A bunch of us veterans are going to be there too to dispense our sage wisdom."

I pretended to check my watch. "Yeah, I should be out of here soon."

"I'll see you there." She spun around and began to walk away, her hips swaying with each movement. I couldn't help but watch her until she reached the double doors and glanced over her shoulders. I froze, unable to look away. Then her eyes darted down to my crotch and back up to my face. She licked her lips, slowly, tortuously, and my head began to spin. A half smile was on her face as she walked out, and the doors clicked shut behind her.

A few short minutes later, I was steering the last of the students out of the gym and into the parking lot. After waving to a few of the parents, I got into my car and started the engine. The world outside raced past in a blur of shapes and colors, but I was unaware of it. All I could think about was the hard-on I still had for my former English teacher.

Kate.

Once I reached my apartment building a few blocks away, I parked the car next to the curb. I took the stairs two at a time, and I was panting by the time I reached my floor. In the apartment, I fumbled for the light and staggered into the room. When I came out of the shower, I pulled on a pair of dark jeans and a button-down shirt. After running my fingers through my hair and spritzing on some cologne, I raced back out the door.

O'Malley's had a cursive neon sign out front and music spilling out of its doors.

Through the glass window, I saw Kate and a few of the other teachers standing in a half-circle near the bar. I parked the car across the street and hurried over, my heart hammering unsteadily the entire time. The smell of alcohol and sweat hit me first, followed quickly by the sound of country music. Then I was pulled into the group of new teachers and patted on the back. Someone shoved me into one of the empty red vinyl booths and handed me a beer. I draped an arm over the back of the booth, and my eyes darted around.

Kate came to sit next to me, her tight red dress really accentuating....well, everything.

She brushed her hand against mine. "You clean up well."

I took a sip of my beer. "So do you."

She tilted her head to the side, and her hand traveled down my chest, stopping on my thigh. "I can't believe you came back to teach. I never would've thought Ricky Morales would be a gym teacher."

I took another sip of my beer and shifted closer to her. "There's a lot you don't know about me."

Kate's hand moved closer to my crotch, and she continued to hold my gaze. "Why don't we go back to my apartment and find out? It's only a few blocks away."

I nodded and downed the rest of my beer.

Kate got out of the booth first and tossed her dark hair behind her ears. Wordlessly, she pushed her way through the crowd, and I followed. My ears were ringing when we stepped outside, and she took my hand in hers. When we reached her apartment building, she took me into the elevator and placed my hand on her chest. I bent my head to kiss her, and she groaned into my mouth.

Holy hell.

I was already as hard as a rock.

She cupped me over the fabric of my jeans and squeezed. Then she rubbed herself against me, and I dug my nails into her waist. By the time the elevator door pinged open, the straps of her dress were lowered, and half of her bra peeked out from underneath. I stood behind her, pressing hot open-mouthed kisses to the back of her neck while she fumbled for her keys. When she finally shoved them into the lock, I gripped her hips and thrust against her.

Kate made a low whimpering sound and dragged me inside. "Not out here."

I was going to explode if I didn't bury myself inside her.

She had no idea how long I'd been waiting for this.

Once we were inside, I kicked the door shut and she launched herself at me, my back colliding with the door. Kate's mouth was hot and eager, and the taste of red wine on her tongue was intoxicating. My hands moved from the back of her neck to her shoulders and down to her ass. I gave it a firm squeeze, the blood still roaring steadily.

She hoisted herself up and wrapped her legs around me.

I fumbled with the zipper on her dress. "You have no idea how many times I've dreamt about this."

"I know," Kate whispered, into my ear. One hand dropped between us, and she began to unbutton my shirt. "I can't wait for you to fuck me, Ricky."

I growled against her skin and carried her over to the kitchen counter. After setting her down, I stepped back and peeled the rest of my shirt off, letting it fall to the floor. Kate's eyes didn't leave my face as she pulled her dress over her head and tossed it aside, leaving her in a lacy black thong and bra.

Holy hell, she was even hotter than I thought with her tanned and toned body.

Teenage me was quivering with anticipation.

Kate reached behind her back and undid the clasps of her bra. "What are you waiting for?"

I stepped in between her legs and lifted her chin. "I want you to remember this. I've waited long enough."

All of those nights spent imagining what she'd feel like, what she'd taste like, didn't do her justice. She clawed at my back, still in her heels as I rubbed my hands up and down her back. I rubbed her over her thin panties and smirked when I realized how wet she was. I pressed kisses all over her face, down her jaw and neck. When I reached her breasts, I took one nipple between my lips and sucked. She threw her head back and moaned.

I moved onto the other nipple, sucking and biting until they were both rock hard.

Her legs tightened around my waist as she rubbed herself against me. Her fingers were deft and quick as she found the zipper to my jeans and pushed it down. Abruptly, I stopped kissing her and stepped out of my jeans, pausing to kick them away. Then I spread her legs open and used my teeth to pull her panties over her legs.

I traced a path along the inside of her thighs. "You smell so good, Kate. And you're so wet."

"Because you make me wet," Kate said, in a low voice. "I hope you've learned a thing or two while you were in college."

I sat back on my legs and looked up at her. "I've been practicing."

Her eyes twinkled, and her breathing was coming out in short puffs. I lifted my head, gripped her hips, and kissed her center. She bucked against me, her fingers moving to the back of my neck. Kate gripped my hair, and a tiny jab of pain burst through me. My tongue darted in between her wet folds, and I sucked. She scooched closer to the edge of the kitchen table and bucked against me.

She tasted better than I thought she would, and the noises she was making made me want her even more. I swiped back and forth, then dragged my tongue up and down, listening for the sound of her whimpers. One hand stayed in my hair, and the other raked over my back, leaving marks there. When her breathing quickened, and she began to chant my name, I held her tighter. Kate exploded, her entire body shaking and writhing with pleasure.

I listened for her heavy breathing and drew back to look at her.

Kate was covered in a thin sheen of sweat, a dazed expression on her face. Abruptly, she sat up and walked over to the desk in the corner. She came back with a long ruler and slapped it against her hand. I stood up and gave her a lazy smile.

"Your performance was good, but it needed something more," she said in a thick voice. "Do you know what you did wrong?"

"No, Ms. Fontana."

She gave me a sultry look. "You and I are just going to have to work closely together to figure that out. Start by playing with my titties."

I covered the distance between us and pinched her nipples. "Like this?"

Kate's eyes widened. "Good. You're a good student."

I swept away the papers on her desk, hoisted her up, and set her down. "Only because I have a good teacher."

Kate purred. "You've always been a promising student."

I kicked her legs apart and stood in between them. "How promising?"

The ruler fell out of her hand as she wrapped her feet around me, drawing me closer. "Incredibly promising."

"Promising enough to fuck you for hours? Promising enough to make it so you can't walk right in the morning?"

Without waiting for a response, I thrust into her, and we both groaned.

She raked her fingers over my back. "Yes."

"Yes, what?" I eased out and slammed back into her, grunting as I did. "I'm going to need you to be a bit more specific, Ms. Fontana. What about my performance needs work?"

Sweat broke out across her forehead. "Nothing."

I thrust in and out of her, in slow practiced strokes. "Really? Are you sure about that?"

She bucked against me, meeting each thrust with one of her own. "Yes."

I linked her fingers over my torso and caged her between my arms, and the back of her desk. "I need you to show me what you want. Show me how to fuck you, Ms. Fontana."

She made a low strangled sound and threw her head back, exposing her long and slender neck. I sank my teeth there, and she hissed. Together, we moved, slowly at first then faster and faster. The desk began to creak and dip as we moved with wild and animal-like abandon. Kate's breasts bounced up and down and rubbed against my chest. I lifted her arms over her head and held them tight.

Kate alternated between panting and moaning my name.

I dropped my head and took one nipple between my teeth. Her chest heaved as I moved onto the other nipple, sucking and lapping. Then I dropped a hand between us and stroked her. She was muttering incoherently now and still marking me with her fingernails. When I shoved one finger in between her wet folds, she buried her face in the crook of my neck. Goosebumps broke out across my flesh as she licked a path from my neck to my jaw and back.

Holy shit.

Kate Fontana knew how to drive a man crazy.

She knew exactly how to touch, how to kiss, how to breathe to get me to want more.

To need more.

I couldn't get enough of her.

Her body writhed and spasmed as another orgasm ripped through her. Once she started breathing normally again, she sat up straighter. I eased out of her and watched her climb off of the desk. She spun around, bent over, and braced her elbows on either side of the desk. Slowly, she shot me a look over her shoulders, the kind that made me feel like I was being set on fire.

From the inside out.

"How about some extra credit, huh?" Kate's voice was low and seductive, and it made me feel like a horny teenager all over again. "Think you can handle that?"

I crossed over to her and positioned myself behind her. "You want me to fuck you from behind?"

Kate held my gaze and didn't look away as I thrust into her. "I want you to fuck me like your life depends on it, like you're trying to teach me a lesson."

I reached for her arm and pinned it over her back. "I'll fuck your brains out."

Over and over I slammed in and out of her until her other arm quivered, and she fell forward, her face resting against the desk. Still, she continued to buck against me. I released her other hand and gripped her hips with both of mine, thrusting like there was no tomorrow. She panted and moaned, screaming my name.

Still, it wasn't enough.

I reached between us and pinched her nipples. "Do you want me to stop?"

"No, harder," Kate said, in a muffled voice. "Don't you dare stop?"

"Going to need you to raise your voice," I said, my chest tightening by now. "I can't hear you over the sound of our fucking."

Kate lifted her head and glanced over her shoulders. "I want you to keep fucking me, as hard as you can."

I slapped her ass and buried my face against her back. "All of your neighbors are going to know."

With that, my thrusts changed, growing wilder and more frantic. Kate's breathing quickened, and another orgasm raced through her, causing her body to shake. It prompted my release, and I exploded inside of her, shaking and jerking with relief.

Kate shifted away from me, her heels clicking as she retrieved a robe and slipped it on. Then she poured us both a generous amount of red wine and tilted her glass in my direction.

"Rest up because we've still got the whole night ahead of us."

Chapter 4

Andrew

by Andrew Morton

I took a swig of my beer and gave Andrew a pointed look. "You're shitting me right now."

Andrew slapped his hand against the counter and reached for a handful of peanuts. "I know it sounds like I am, but I'm really not. You should've seen her."

I glanced around the crowded bar, covered in a thin layer of smoke and packed to the brim with people, all reeking of alcohol and sweat while low music pumped in the background. Now and again, when the bell above the door rang, I glanced up, and my heart did a little nose dive when her familiar head of hair didn't appear.

I was a fucking idiot.

Beth wasn't going to show up.

She'd made it clear, but a part of me still clung to the idea that she would anyway.

Like some kind of lovesick moron.

What was the matter with me anyway?

Andrew leaned forward, his smirk stretching from ear to ear. "Do you remember that story I told you about how she gave me a handy on the subway?"

"Yeah, underneath your coat," I muttered, pausing to take another swig of my beer. "I still can't believe you did that in a crowded subway."

Andrew chuckled. "I thought that old lady was going to have a stroke, and the woman with the kid....man, she looked like she was going to kill me."

"No one really wants to see that kind of thing," I pointed out, signaling to the bartender for another drink. "How do you get Angelica to agree to these things anyway?"

"They're her ideas most of the time," Andrew replied in between sips of his drink. "I have to say, out of all the people I've been with, she's by the far the kinkiest and wildest."

I stared down at my drink and swirled it around. "Okay."

"When we did it on the beach the other day, we almost got caught a few times, and she didn't even care," Andrew said in a lower voice. "There we are, with my swimming trunks around my ankles, and her tits are bouncing up and down, and she didn't give one single fuck."

I took a long sip of my drink. "Were you doing it in the car or something?"

Andrew shook his head. "In the mouth of that cave, and she was fingering herself the entire time."

A jolt went through me at the image, and I had to shift from one side to the other. A loud cacophony of voices rose from one side of the room, and I glanced over to see a group of women in feather boas, printed t-shirts, and plastic tiaras on their heads. Andrew followed my gaze and clapped me on the back.

"You should go over there. They look like they know how to have fun."

I wrenched my gaze away and turned my attention back to my drink. "They look like too much drama."

"Come on," Andrew groaned and sat up straighter on the stool. "You're no fun ever since Beth came into the picture. She's got you by the balls, man."

My grip on my drink tightened. "She does not."

Except we both knew I was lying.

As much as I hated to admit it, I couldn't so much as look at another woman without thinking of Beth. Even hearing about Andrew and Angelica's wild sexcapades wasn't having the effect it usually did. Whenever I heard about the wild adventures they got up to, it usually inspired me to get into some trouble of my own.

"Do you see that blonde girl on the far right of the booth? Angelica and I fucked her."

I stopped with the bottle halfway to my lips. "What?"

Andrew nodded, a little too eagerly. "Yeah, we went to this sex club a few weeks ago. They have these like orgies, and you're basically high and having fun, and that blonde was checking me out."

I raised an eyebrow and twisted to face him. "Angelica didn't get pissed?"

Beth would've ripped me a new one.

Andrew chuckled. "Not only did she not get pissed. She actually encouraged me to make a move, and when we went to a private room upstairs, she stood and watched. I was balls deep in this girl when Angelica got down on her knees and started sucking on her tits."

"See, I feel like you're making this shit up."

Because there was no way he'd gotten that lucky with a woman as hot as Angelica.

There had to be a catch.

Andrew clapped me on the back. "I'm not. She's wild man, and get this, she actually wants to try a threesome next."

I took a sip of my drink, and it burned a path down my throat. "What was it that you did with the blonde then?"

Andrew signaled for another drink. "She means with another man. She wants to be fucked by two men at the same time."

I blinked. "And you're okay with this?"

Andrew nodded. "Yeah."

"Bullshit. You hate it when another man looks at a woman you're dating, and you usually want to put their face through a wall. "

Andrew shrugged. "I wouldn't mind as long as it was someone I knew and trusted."

I snorted and took another sip of my drink. "Yeah, good luck with that."

Andrew turned so he was facing me directly. "So, what do you say?"

I rose to my feet and ran a hand over my face. "What?"

Andrew leaned in closer so I could hear him above the noise. "Which hole do you prefer?"

I choked back a laugh. "You're not actually propositioning me, are you?"

Andrew stood up, and we weaved in and out of the groups of people until we reached the bathroom. Inside, I took a urinal on the far left, and he chose one in the middle. The three stalls were wide open and empty, and a man was admiring his reflection in the glass mirror underneath bright fluorescent lighting. After I was done, I zipped up and went to wash my hands, feeling Andrew's gaze on me the whole time.

When we stepped out, the noise hit me first, followed closely by the smell.

We picked our way through the crowd until we were back at the bar, and the bartender immediately brought us another round. "What time is Angelica getting here anyway?"

Andrew leaned against the counter opposite me. "Eager to get started, huh? She'll be here soon, and we can go back to our place."

I took a long sip of my drink and grimaced. "I don't think that's a good idea, man."

No matter how much I desperately wanted to forget Beth.

A good fuck was exactly what I needed, and it would be even more fun if I were to spice things up, just to keep my mind from wandering. But Andrew was one of my oldest friends, and no matter how hot and sexy Angelica was, I knew I couldn't risk our friendship like that.

Not even for the rare opportunity to fuck her brains out.

Angelica arrived a short while later, and Andrew was still making his case, growing more and more animated by the minute. He was in the middle of describing, in graphic detail, all of the ways we could have fun when she walked right up to us and placed a hand on his arm. She whispered something in his ear, and Andrew stopped talking. He picked up his drink and walked away without a backward glance. With a smile, Angelica took my hand and led me out into the middle of the bar, where a few people were swaying to the music.

She placed both hands on her hips and gave them a little extra sway. "I know you think I'm hot."

I kept my hands on her hips and tried to focus on her face, not the cleavage that was showing through her tight top. "It doesn't matter. I'm not going to jeopardize my friendship with Drew."

Angelica gave me another smile and spun around. She pressed her ass against me and wriggled. I choked back a growl and tried to move my hands away. Immediately, she took both and helped me run them down the length of her smooth, petite body. Then she twisted an arm behind her back and laced her fingers through my hair. I blew out a breath and tried not to think of how good it felt to have her pressed against me.

And to have her firm ass against my crotch.

The way she moved made me want to take her then and there.

Angelica stopped swinging her hips and spun around to face me. Without saying a word, she took my hand in hers and dragged me off to a secluded part of the club, where there were no eyes or ears. As soon as she did, she pushed me up against the wall and started kissing me. Instinct took over, and I responded. One hand went to the back of her neck, and the other stroked her butt. She made a low whimpering sound and rubbed herself against me. Through the thin fabric of her shirt, I could feel her nipples poking me.

Holy shit.

It was no wonder she had Andrew wrapped around her finger.

I was already hard for her.

Her hand darted between us to cup me. I growled into her mouth and gripped the back of her head. I gave it a firm tug, and she made a low whimpering sound in her throat. Then she rubbed herself against me and all of my protest melted away. Every last fear and every last insecurity didn't exist under her expert touch.

When she drew back to look at me, I buried my face in the crook of her neck.

She smelled like strawberries and champagne.

I sank my teeth into her neck, and she hissed. Her hand darted underneath my shirt to untuck it. Her fingers were warm and sure against my flushed skin. When they ducked underneath my boxer shorts to grip me, I knew I was a goner. I breathed her in and realized I wanted to completely bury myself in her.

Consequences be damned.

Angelica licked her lips and pressed hot, open-mouthed kisses down the side of my neck and over my jaw. "How do you feel about it now?"

I stopped sucking on her neck and pulled back to look at her. "When do we leave?"

Her green eyes lit up in amusement as she took my hand and dragged me behind her. We wove in and out of the throngs of people until we spotted Andrew by the front door, a shit-eating grin on his face. He kissed Angelica on her way past.

Outside, Angelica shoved me into the backseat and got in beside me.

Andrew got into the front and started the engine. "This is going to be a hell of a night."

"I'm going to give you a hell of a show, baby," Angelica said, pausing to straddle me. She gave him a sultry look over her shoulders before she twisted her arms behind her back. I heard a familiar snap, and Angelica leaned forward to press my face between her breasts. My hands went down to her legs, and I lifted her skirt so it pooled around her waist.

Andrew's eyes darted between the streets and us.

Angelica cupped my face between her hands and kissed me, hard enough to make my lips bruise. Then she ground against me, and a jolt of molten hot desire raced through me. I thrust upward and rubbed myself against her soaking-wet panties. She made another low noise that sounded like music to my ears. I snuck one hand under her shirt and squeezed her nipples. Angelica rocked back and forth against me, tossing her long hair back over her shoulders.

The car came to a screeching halt outside their apartment building.

A door clicked open, and Angelica pulled me out, stumbling behind her. In the elevator, she and Andrew made out while I fondled her, a thick and heavy fog of desire settling over me. I was dry-humping her while Andrew sucked on her nipples. Angelica twisted one arm behind her back to grab the back of my neck, and the other cupped Andrew over his jeans.

The door pinged open, and we were barely able to pull ourselves away.

Angelica giggled as I held onto her waist. With a smirk, Andrew pushed the key into the lock and kicked the door open. As soon as he did, Angelica spun around to draw me into her arms and another searing kiss. I smiled and bit down on her bottom lip, eliciting a groan. Bright light danced in my field of vision as we staggered through the apartment until we reached the bedroom. There, Angelica pushed me down onto the bed and began to peel off her clothes.

Holy fuck.

I was having some kind of insane wet dream, and I didn't want it to end.

She wriggled as she pushed down her skirt, revealing smooth hips and a white thong that barely covered anything. With a smile, she spun around, offering me ample view of her ass as she kicked off her underwear and peeled off her shirt. When she turned around to face me again, I was already touching myself.

Angelica pouted and climbed onto the bed. "Having fun without me?"

"I would never," I replied, in a thick voice. "How do you want me?"

"Just relax, baby." Angelica lifted my arms over my head and lowered herself onto me. Once I filled her to the hilt, she began to buck and moan. My heart was pounding in my ears now, and I could barely hear anything over her heavy breathing, and my frantic groaning. Then Andrew walked in, completely naked, and sat down on the couch opposite the bed.

He began to stroke himself while watching us.

I lifted my gaze, and our eyes met.

Andrew's lips lifted into a smile as he touched two fingers to his brow in a mock salute. Then his expression changed, and he began to pump himself more vigorously. I swung my gaze back to Angelica, who was rocking back and forth against me, her tits bouncing up and down. With a smile, I raised my head and took one nipple between my lips. She moaned and threw her head back. I moved to her other nipple and pushed one finger in between her wet folds.

She was soaking wet.

Fucking hell.

She was a beast, a sexy and dirty little beast.

Out of the corner of my eye, I saw a flash of movement, and Andrew appeared in my field of vision. I lifted my knees and thrust upward. Angelica glanced over her shoulders and gave Andrew a searing kiss. After positioning himself behind her ass, he thrust in one quick move. Angelica's eyes widened, and she muttered something incoherent under her breath.

Andrew adjusted his knees, so all three of us could move at the same time.

Angelica was touching herself and pressing her breasts together. I was focused on how it felt to be balls deep inside of her, to have her juices all over my cock. Angelica swayed against each movement and each thrust, her forehead shiny with sweat by now. I reached for her hands and placed them on my chest. Then I pressed her breasts together and nibbled on her nipples. She threw her head back, and Andrew sank his teeth into her neck.

None of us said anything as the bed dipped and creaked.

Soon, our heavy breathing and sweat filled the room, and it was all I could think about. Angelica was making noises I had never heard a woman make before, and she was moving in ways that surprised and thrilled me. I had no idea a woman could stand to be fucked so thoroughly and so deeply by two men at the same time.

It was deeply erotic and thrilling to have a front row seat to her coming undone.

Andrew yanked on her hair. "How does it feel, baby? Is being fucked by two men everything you wanted it to be?"

"Fuck, yes," Angelica breathed, her pupils dilating. "You're both so big."

With that, she dropped her head and captured my lips with hers. I bit down on her bottom lip and let my tongue swirl around her mouth. She tasted like wine and cherry bubblegum, and it was a heady mixture I couldn't get enough of. When I cupped her breasts, Angelica panted and wrenched her lips away.

She threw her head back, gave a few more thrusts, and exploded.

The force of her orgasm ripped through her, prompting her body to writhe and shake with pleasure. Sweat broke out across her forehead and down the sides of her face. When she was done, she was still moving against me. She twisted an arm over her head to play with Andrew's hair. Then she bent down to press hot, open-mouthed kisses all over my chest. When I eased out of her, and she took me in her mouth, all it took was one look.

One look for me to violently came inside of her mouth.

She kept licking and sucking until my vision cleared, and I was no longer shaking. Afterward, I lay on the mattress while Andrew lined up behind Angelica and continued to fuck her from behind. He thrust in and out of her while I watched, idly touching myself the entire time. Angelica's body caved again as another orgasm ripped through her, prompting Andrew's own release. The two of them shouted as he emptied himself into her and grew still.

Angelica draped herself on the mattress next to me when she was done. "You hungry?"

I twisted to face her. "I could eat you."

Angelica smiled. "I meant food."

"That too."

"Looks like he's ready for round two," Andrew said into her neck. "What do you think, babe?"

Chapter 5

Keith

By Keith Palahi

I could tell she kept herself in shape.

Sandy was telling the group a little about her short-lived stint as a college volleyball player, and I hung on to her every word. When everyone else was talking, I tuned them out, but when it came time for Sandy, I sat up straighter and couldn't keep my eyes off her. She was wearing a pair of tight pink yoga pants that clung to her firm and round ass, a tank top that showed off her flat and toned stomach, and a belly button ring that glistened underneath florescent lighting. When she shifted, my eyes were drawn to her long and shapely legs.

I wondered how they would feel wrapped around me while I buried myself in her.

Or how it would feel to have them thrown over my shoulders while I had her screaming in pleasure.

Sandy looked like she was a screamer, the kind who called your name out over and over again while you thrust in and out of her. While a part of me felt like I should hide how she made me feel, especially considering we were all part of the same gym, and the same ab and core exercises group, the other part of me couldn't help it.

I'd moved to the city months ago, and my time was spent alternating between my boring corporate job, and the gym. And between the two, I much preferred the gym, even if I did have to endure the get-to-know-you portion of each new class. Up until a few weeks ago, I'd barely paid attention, glancing at my phone the whole time. But the minute Sandy walked in, with her midnight black curls that framed her face, full sumptuous lips, and a body that was begging to be fucked, I'd begun to look forward to this part of the evening.

Hell, I even tried to choose the machines that were closest to her, and it was starting to pay off. Two weeks ago, she'd started to notice me. Now, every evening when we came in, she offered me a bright smile and a once-over. She and I hadn't ever spoken, but I was sure that if we did, she'd see what she was missing out on.

All I had to do was bide my time until the right moment.

And that right moment was today.

Toward the end of her introduction, when she announced it was her last class, and she'd be moving to California, my stomach dropped. I spent the rest of the talking portion staring at her with a furrow between my brows. After class, I waited till most of the other people were busy before I walked up to her. When I stopped in front of her, I gave her a slow once-over, starting with the tips of her toes and ending with the top of her head.

"I know we've never spoken before, but I just wanted to tell you that I think you're gorgeous."

Sandy's whole face lit up, and her hazel eyes were kind and warm when she looked at me. "Thanks. So are you."

"It's a shame you're moving away. Having someone like you around, strong and dedicated I mean, has been really helpful. You've really inspired me."

"You don't look like you need it." Sandy nodded in the direction of my toned arms. "You seem like you do a good job on your own."

"It helps to have some extra motivation," I maintained.

Sandy nodded and pushed her hair out of her eyes. "Of course. That's part of the reason why I'm moving. There's more opportunities for people like me in California."

"I wish you the best of luck," I replied with a smile. "You sure are going to be missed."

"I wish you'd come up to say hello sooner, Keith." Sandy pouted and placed both hands on her hips. "We could've been good friends."

I shrugged. "Timing."

Sandy nodded, an inscrutable expression on her face. "True."

With one final wave, I walked away, and I felt her eyes on me the whole time. Thanking God I was wearing my good pair of basketball shorts and a top that stretched over my muscles, I was smiling to myself. I went into the shower stall and thought of her the whole time. I thought of her toned muscles while I lathered up some soap and waited for the hot water. I thought of her as I ran the bar of soap over my body, imagining her long and capable fingers instead.

Then I pictured her on her hands and knees in front of me as I thrust in and out of her mouth. I saw myself with my back pressed against the wall while water swirled around us, her lips around my cock. When I was as hard as a rock, I tried to think of something else and ended up reaching for the shampoo bottle. With my eyes closed, I ran my fingers through my hair and braced my hands on either side of the shower.

I was taking several deep breaths when I heard the bathroom door creak open.

Frowning, I washed the soap out of my eyes and spun around to see Sandy through the glass stall. She was looking at something in the mirror. Then she glanced around and pulled her tank top off, revealing a lacy bra underneath. She lifted her gaze, and our eyes met in the mirror. One corner of her mouth turned into a smile as she wriggled out of her yoga pants and left them in a heap on the floor.

Sandy was in nothing but her bra and panties when she crossed over to me.

Holy fuck.

Bitch had bigger balls than I did.

She pushed the stall open and stepped in. "I was thinking we can still get to know each other."

I pulled her toward me and lifted her chin. "What a strange coincidence. You were just on my mind."

Sandy glanced down and back up, her smile widening. "I can see that."

In one quick move, I spun us around, so her back was pressed against the wall, and I had my arms on either side of her. "You look like you like a good fuck."

Sandy peeled off her wet panties and bra and kicked them away. "Why don't you find out?"

I lowered my head and inches away from her mouth, I stopped. "I plan on it."

With that, I captured her lips with mine and growled. Sandy responded by bringing her arms up over my neck and threading her fingers through my hair. I kept one hand on the wall, and the other ran up and down her side, prompting Sandy to shiver in anticipation. Hot water continued to swirl and fall around us. When we were both out of breath, and the need for air became too great, I wrenched my lips away and pressed kisses down her jaw and over her neck. She gripped the back of my neck tighter, making me hiss in response.

Sandy threw her head back and moaned. "Don't be such a tease."

Smirking, I lowered myself onto my knees and glanced up at her. Then I shoved my wet hair out of my eyes and gripped her hips. She made another choked sound and ran a hand over my face. I kissed a path along the inside of her thighs, smiling when goosebumps broke out across her flesh. Slowly, I lifted my gaze to hers and held it. Sandy blinked and shoved her wet hair out of her face.

She was breathing heavily now, and it was the best sound I'd ever heard.

Up until I pried her legs open and pressed a kiss against her clit.

Sandy moaned and bucked against me. "Fuck, that feels good."

I kept one hand on her waist, and the other snaked up her chest. "We're just getting started."

Without warning, I pinched one nipple and then the other. She pushed herself off the wall and whispered my name, a prayer on her lips. My hands traveled back down, and I hoisted her up, so her legs were on my shoulders, leaving her pussy exposed and at eye level.

With a growl, I used two fingers to push her wet folds apart and blew hot air there.

Sandy shivered and gripped the back of my neck. "Please."

"Please what?"

Sandy looked down at me and bit her lip. "I want your mouth on me."

My tongue darted out, and I licked a path from right to left. "Like this?"

Sandy jerked and exhaled. "More."

I licked another path, slowly dragging my tongue from up to down. "You mean like this?"

Sandy bucked against my mouth. "More."

I chuckled and plunged my tongue completely, licking and sucking at her wet folds. She was soaking wet, and while I dragged my tongue back and forth, I tasted her, really tasted her, and realized it was the best thing I'd ever tried. Her hips didn't stop moving once the entire time, grinding against me. Her mouth was parted, and she kept calling out my name as if that was going to make me go any faster.

But I had no intention of rushing this.

Since we had the gym all to ourselves, I had every intention of fucking her till she couldn't stand.

Till she couldn't breathe.

Till she couldn't bend over without imagining my dick inside of her.

I wanted Sandy to think of me in California and miss me so much that the ache between her legs became unbearable.

I growled and shook my head back and forth. Sandy's breathing quickened, and her hands fell to her sides. She was bucking frantically now, unashamedly chasing her high without abandon. When she did lose control, and her entire body jerked in response, I only drove my tongue in further. Over and over I dragged out her release, wanting her to feel every last inch of it.

She blew out a harsh breath when she stopped shaking and pulled me to my feet.

She kissed me soundly then, her lips parting to allow me access into her mouth. I tasted the flavored water on her tongue, and I wanted more. Before I could deepen the kiss, she pushed herself off the wall and gave me a hooded look. Then she lowered herself onto her knees and pushed me against the wall. My heart was pounding in my ears as she placed one hand on either of my thighs and smiled. She licked her lips and pressed her face closer to my throbbing cock.

Then she ran her smooth, deft tongue along the outer shaft.

She licked it a few more times and then her hand came up to cup my balls. I jerked, a powerful jolt coursing through me. Sandy smiled up at me before taking me in her mouth. Panting, I gripped the back of her head, eased out, and slammed back in. She made a low choking sound in the back of her throat, and her eyes rolled to the back of her head. Then she balanced herself upright and let me thrust in and out of her. The noises she was making were unlike anything I'd ever heard.

But I couldn't bring myself to care that someone might hear us.

All I cared about was being able to thrust in and out of her mouth while she continued to make those sexy noises, acting like I was the only man in the world to ever make her feel this way. Sandy braced her hands on either side of my thighs and moaned. A low thrumming started in the back of my head, growing stronger and stronger. Before I erupted, I stopped thrusting and yanked her head back. Her eyes watered, but she didn't say anything when I drew her to her feet and kissed her.

She kissed me back with just as much enthusiasm and fire.

Breathing heavily now, I pushed myself off the wall. "I don't want our fun to be over too soon."

Sandy gave me a slow, sultry smile. "Is that so?"

"Stand with your stomach pressed against the wall," I said. "And lift your arms over your head. Don't move until I tell you to."

Sandy's smile remained in place as she did what she was told.

"Good girl. You like being told what to do, don't you?"

I stroked myself when she lifted her arms on either side of her and spared me a look over her shoulders. Her eyes darkened when she followed my hands and saw what I was doing. "Need some help with that?"

I took a step forward and shook my head. "No."

With that, I bridged the distance between us and rubbed myself against her back. She clenched the muscles of her ass and breathed a sigh of impatience. I pressed my lips against her neck, and she reacted to my proximity. I started kissing the back of her neck while she made low mewling sounds. Then I used one hand to hold her arms tight, and the other reached out and pressed her breasts together. Sandy threw her head back and wriggled her hips.

"You feel so good," I said into her skin. "Tell me, Sandy. How many times have you been fucked like this?"

"Never like this." Sandy breathed, her voice catching towards the end. "Ever."

I raised an eyebrow and continued to rub my dick against her ass. "No one has ever teased you like this? No one has ever made you stand like this while they tortured you?"

Sandy shook her head, sending droplets of water in every direction. "No one."

I took her bottom lobe between my teeth. "We're going to have to fix that."

Without waiting for a response, I used both hands to grip her hips. After positioning myself behind her, I thrust. Sandy twisted her arms behind her back to grab the back of my neck. I let her as I eased out and slammed back into her wet juices. She bucked, slowly at first then faster and faster, her movements growing wild and a little frantic. I unlinked her arms from around my neck and pressed them against the wall. While I fucked her, I held her hands on top of her head, knowing how much she'd enjoy it.

Women like Sandy liked being controlled.

They liked realizing what they could or couldn't do.

And they definitely liked a man who took charge of their sex life and brought them to their knees. Before we left for the night, I had every intention of having Sandy screaming my name and eager for the release only I could give her. Growling, I used both hands to hold her arms up, so they were pinned on either side of her. Sandy's breath quickened as we rocked back and forth against each other. The door to the showers creaked open, and we heard a pair of footsteps.

I placed a hand over Sandy's mouth and brought my mouth to her ear. "Don't make a sound, or I'll only fuck you harder."

Sandy nodded, a little too eagerly.

"Keep fucking me," I whispered, before tugging on her bottom lobe again. "Whoever is out there, they don't matter."

Sandy nodded again and continued to grind against me.

Her firm and tight ass kept going while I slammed in and out of her. I was knee-deep in her and trying to hold back my own moans. Then I heard the sound of a faucet being turned on, and I stopped. A heartbeat later, the footsteps receded, and I breathed into her smooth and supple skin. Once I was sure they were gone, I eased out of Sandy and spun her around.

Her mouth fell open in surprise, and her breasts were as hard as pebbles as she wrapped her arms around my neck. "You're so fucking hot when you take charge and boss me around."

"Keep your arms around my neck and wrap your legs around my waist," I grunted. "And prepare for the fuck of a lifetime."

The words barely left my lips before I hoisted her up and rammed into her. Sandy raked her fingers over my back, stopping to give my ass a firm squeeze. Then she kept one hand there, and the other gripped the back of my neck. She tightened her grip, sending dual waves of pain and pleasure through me. Water continued to slide and swirl underneath us, making our bodies slick.

I crushed Sandy between the wall and my body and continued to thrust.

First in slow and practiced strokes and then harder and harder, my movements designed to drive her absolutely wild.

Just like I'd been wanting to do for months.

Her chest heaved, and her pulse quickened. Sandy dug her fingers into my shoulders, and I buried my face in her neck. She threw her head back and cried out my name, over and over, until it reverberated inside of my head. As she climbed down from her high, I gave a few more quick thrusts and grunted.

My entire body jerked and exploded while I spilled into her.

Sandy's legs were still secured around my waist, still bucking wildly. By the time I caught my breath, she was running her fingers through my hair and smiling. Slowly, I set her back down on her feet, and she leaned against the wall. I draped myself against her and waited for my breathing to settle.

Sandy gave me another searing kiss and stepped out of the shower.

From behind the glass stall, I watched her pull on her clothes, sans panties.

She blew me a kiss over her shoulders and walked away.

After drying off, I pulled on my own clothes, whistling to myself as I did. Outside, the receptionist behind the counter had a knowing smirk on his face. "Nice."

I scratched the back of my head. "About what you may or may not have heard—"

He held a hand up and leaned against the counter. "Don't worry about it, man. Do you think you're the only clients to ever fuck in that shower? You're not the first, and you won't be the last."

I cleared my throat. "Thanks."

After giving me a high five, he went back to his phone, and we never talked about it again.

Chapter 6

Carl

By Carl Rasmussen

"I can't wait to marry you tomorrow," Shelly whispered, pausing to lock her fingers behind my head. "Do you have any idea how excited I am?"

I leaned forward and pressed a kiss to her lips. "As excited as I am."

Shelly giggled and leaned into my touch. "I wish we didn't have to wait till tomorrow."

I smiled and drew her into my arms. "We don't have to. You know I love you, Shelly. Nothing is going to change that."

She drew back to look at me. "Not even sleeping with me before we got married?"

I cupped her face in my hands and looked into her eyes. "Nothing is going to change how I feel about you. You're the first woman I've ever wanted to have sex with, and I hope you're the last."

Because I couldn't imagine feeling this way about anyone else.

Like I was on fire from the inside out.

Shelly and I had known each other for years, but whenever she was around, I felt like a horny and love-struck teenager. I wanted to be around her all the time, to hear her laugh and see her face light up with that familiar smile of hers.

And I desperately wanted to have sex with her, to spread her legs open and bury myself in her.

My cock twitched at the thought of her wet juices.

The past few weeks were torture, having to hold her close and smell her and not being able to drag her into the nearest room and peel her clothes off. Still, we had both decided to wait, believing that God would bless our marriage further if we did. Unfortunately, the longer we stood there, in the middle of my hotel suite, the more difficult I found it to remember why we had to wait.

And the harder I got.

I knew she felt it because when she shifted, her breath quickened. Shelly withdrew her arms and took an involuntary step back. "I love you too, Carl. You know I do, but we...we shouldn't."

I took a step forward. "Why not?"

Shelly shook her head, wisps of red hair escaping from her bun. "It'll be more special if we wait."

I took a step back and retrieved the schedule book from on top of the table. "Have you seen this?"

Every hour of our day tomorrow was accounted for from the minute we woke up until we closed our eyes. Given how hectic our wedding day was going to be, I was worried we weren't going to have the time to have sex, much less the energy. Shelly flipped through the pages, her frown deepening and deepening. She took the book out of my hands and carried it over to the couch. Then she sat down and tucked her legs under her.

I released a deep breath and stood up straighter. "Come on, tell me you aren't looking at that and seeing what I'm seeing. I want you, Shelly, and tomorrow we're going to be man and wife. One less day isn't going to hurt."

Nor was it going to make a big difference in the grand scheme of things.

But I had no idea if it was my hormones or my logic talking.

Someone knocked on the hotel door, and I went to open it. A young man with dark hair peeking out from under his hat and wearing a black and green uniform stood behind a table. With a smile, he wheeled it inside, only stopping to unscrew the lid on the champagne. He nodded and retrieved a tray from under the tablecloth.

"Compliments of the hotel."

"Thank you," I murmured, before reaching into my pocket. After handing him a tip, I walked him back to the door and slammed it shut. "It's a sign."

Shelly was standing up now and running a hand over her face. "Yes, you're right."

I poured some champagne into two glasses. "I am?"

Shelly nodded. "You are."

When I handed her the glass, I tried to hide the tremor in my hands. Shelly downed the whole thing and signaled for me to add some more. Then she began to undress, starting with the buttons of her jeans and revealing a pair of white cotton panties underneath. After kicking her jeans away, her fingers moved to the buttons of her shirt. She undid one after the other in quick succession, revealing a matching white bra.

Fucking hell.

I didn't think I could ever get used to seeing her like this, so vulnerable and sexy.

And all mine.

I downed my own drink, but it took me a few tries to peel off my own clothes. By then, Shelly was blushing all over. I crossed over to her and tilted her head back. "We've seen each other like this before."

Just a few days ago, her mom had almost caught us going at it in the closet.

Shelly had been in a similar pair of panties and bra, and she'd been panting and pawing at my back. I'd been rubbing myself against her and trying to remember all the reasons why we had to wait. When Shelly's hand had reached between us to cup me, I'd almost snapped then and there. I had positioned myself at her entrance and was getting ready to thrust when we heard her mother's voice.

Since then, I have been careful.

But I didn't want to be anymore.

After two years of dreaming what it would be like to be with her, of imagining her hair between my fingers and her soft skin pressed against mine, I didn't have to anymore. Shelly's lips lifted in a smile, and I kissed her. She kissed me back with just as much fervor and passion, and my hands moved down to her hips. I hoisted her up and carried her into the suite's bedroom. When I set her down on the bed, we were still kissing, and Shelly was rubbing herself against me.

Holy shit.

It was going to be over before it even started with the way she was touching me.

Every inch of me reacted to her touch. I was buzzing like electricity coursing through my veins. Shelly linked her fingers over my neck and linked her feet behind my back. My breath hitched in my throat as she nipped on my bottom lip, and my mouth parted. Her tongue darted in, and we began a sensual battle for dominance with Shelly whimpering the entire time.

How was I supposed to hold out when she held me like that?

Holy hell.

I growled into the kiss and pinned her arms over her head. Shelly wrenched her lips away and threw her head to the side. I pressed hot, open-mouthed kisses down the side of her face, over her jaw, down her neck, and stopped at the dip of her chest. Heart hammering unsteadily against my chest, I helped her sit up and fumbled with the clasp on her bra.

Why were my hands so sweaty?

"Do you need some help?" Her voice was low and breathy, and she was staring at me through hooded eyes. It made me want her even more. I swallowed past the lump in my throat and wiped my palms against the sheets. Then I tried again, slower this time, and when I finally undid the clasp, my heart almost stopped.

Shelly shivered as her perky round breasts spilled forward.

There was a slight tremor as I reached between us and cupped them in my hands. "How's this?"

Shelly released a shaky breath and leaned into my touch. "It feels amazing."

I pressed her breasts together and licked my lips. "They're so soft."

Shelly's hands went to the back of my neck, and she pushed my head down. "Taste them."

I snapped to attention. "What?"

"I want you to taste me, Carl," Shelly whispered, her voice rising toward the end. "I want to feel every last part of you on my skin. We've waited long enough."

As soon as the words left her lips, I kissed her again, harder this time.

As if I was trying to drown in her.

She fell backward against the mattress, and I loomed over her. Shelly's hands fell to her sides as she grabbed a fistful of the sheets. I rubbed my hands up and down her arms as she twisted and squirmed, my name falling steadily from her lips. When I stopped rubbing her arms, I thrust one hand through her hair, and the other traced a path down the slope of her chest.

I stopped at the curve of her hips and dug my nails there. "Are you sure?"

Shelly wriggled against me. "I want to be yours, Carl. Completely."

I nudged her legs open and buried my face in her neck. My heart was pounding unevenly as I struggled to catch my breath. Slowly, I kissed a path down her chest, pausing to take one nipple between my teeth. While I sucked and bit, one hand darted between us to stroke me. Her bare fingers on my cock felt amazing like I was going to explode into a million pieces.

I twitched and thrust against her hand.

She smiled against my skin and continued to run her fingers up and down my shaft. "I've been doing my homework too, you know...prepare."

I moved onto her other nipple and groaned. "Me, too."

Shelly arched her back when one hand drifted down to stroke her center. "You're a good student."

I let out a long breath. "So are you."

Shelly held me in a firm grip and ran her hands up and down the length of my cock, driving me more and more wild. "How's this? Do you want me to do anything differently?"

I shook my head and one finger darted in between her wet folds. "Not at all."

Her hips rose off the mattress, and she cried out. "Oh, Carl....mmmm, that feels so good."

I pushed another finger in and waited for her muscles to relax. "How's this?"

While I waited for her to adjust to the feel of my fingers, I imagined kissing a path down to her stomach. I saw myself settled in between her legs, with my tongue pressed against her center. Already, the smell of her wet juices was driving me crazy, far better than anything I could've dreamed up or imagined. Shelly bucked against my fingers, and something in me snapped.

I sank my teeth into her neck and began to pump her with my fingers.

Her grip on my cock relaxed and then tightened again. She moved her hands up and down at an alarming speed, eliciting grunt after grunt. I used my free hand to grip the back of her neck and tilted her head back. Her eyes were half-closed, and she had a thin sheen of sweat on her forehead. I had known her for years, and I knew she had never looked more beautiful.

Nor more powerful.

Shelly's body shook and writhed as she rode out her orgasm. Her skin broke out into goosebumps as she arched her back again and released the sheets. She was panting and writhing when I removed my fingers and licked them. Shelly lifted her gaze, and her expression was hungry and eager when she saw me licking her juices off my fingers. Abruptly, she sat up and drew me closer, crushing her mouth to mine.

I tasted her yearning and desperation as if it were my own.

She raked her fingers over my back, leaving marks all over my flushed skin again. I rubbed myself against her, and it made her want me even more. Shelly kept one hand on the back of my neck, and the other drifted between us until it stopped at the waistband of her underwear. In one quick move, she peeled it off and stopped kissing me long enough to kick it off. I crushed her to me and tried to ignore the tightness in my chest.

Shelly was muttering incoherently when I kissed a path down her chest and stopped at her stomach. Slowly, I lifted my gaze and held hers as I nudged her legs open. Her mouth parted, and color crept up her neck and cheeks as I began to press hot kisses along the inside of her thighs. She tasted like butter and coconut lotion, and I was addicted.

Until I reached her center, and I knew I was done for.

My tongue darted in, and I licked a path from right to left, pausing to glance up at her. Shelly's hips were off the mattress, and both of her arms were by her sides. She gripped a handful of the sheets and moaned, the sound like music to my ears. I dug my nails into her waist and plunged my tongue in further, knowing how to move because of all of the videos and articles I'd read. I'd spent the better part of the past few months trying to learn everything I could about sex.

Including how to please a woman.

Being able to put it to good use felt far better than anything I could've dreamed up.

Or anything I read.

Shelly was totally and completely at my mercy, and I was enjoying every minute. Every moan that fell from her lips, every flutter of her hands, and every touch of my skin was driving me more and more crazy. As I began to shake my head back and forth, lapping up her wet juices, Shelly's hands went to the back of my neck.

She wound her fingers through my hair and pushed me closer. Then she began to grind against me, the sound of her pants filling the room.

She was sexy as fuck.

I didn't want her to stop.

I kept one hand on her waist, and the other moved up to flick her nipples. I played with one and then the other, so they were both as hard as pebbles. Shelly's release loomed closer and closer. When the force of her orgasm ripped through her, Shelly cried out and pulled me up. She kissed me while her body writhed and shook, and I tasted bliss on her tongue. When she stopped shaking, her hand dropped between us, and she wrapped her hand around me.

Before I knew what was happening, she had me positioned at her entrance.

I placed my hands on either side of the headboard, glanced down at her, and smiled. "This is it."

Shelly wriggled underneath me and linked her feet over my torso. "I love you, Carl."

I pressed my forehead to hers. "I love you too, Shelly."

With that, I entered her with one quick thrust. Shelly grew absolutely still, and I waited for her muscles to contract. She was tight and wet, but I knew how important it was to ease her into it. I lowered my head to kiss her and nibbled on her bottom lip. After a long moment, she sighed and wriggled her hips. I thrust in further, and she whimpered.

Another heartbeat later, I thrust in further.

When I was at the hilt, I eased out and slammed back into her.

Shelly's muscles contracted as she called out my name. I kept my arms on either side of the headboard and circled my hips. Her hands moved down my back and stopped at my ass. She gave it a firm squeeze and sighed. I slammed back into her and waited.

Holy fuck.

I couldn't believe this was finally happening, and in a hotel suite the night before our wedding of all places.

It felt strange to be inside of Shelly, to know that there were no more boundaries between us, but it also didn't feel like it was enough.

I wanted more.

I needed more.

Shelly shifted, and her hands curled into fists on either side of her. She lifted her knees as I eased in and out of her, in slow and even strokes. Each touch, each kiss, each thrust brought us closer and closer. It wasn't long before Shelly was completely relaxed and began to buck against me. One hand fell to her shoulders, and the other moved to her breasts. I played with them until Shelly began to grow restless, her movements jerky and uncoordinated.

I felt my own release build, looming closer and closer.

When Shelly used her legs to draw me closer, and her nipples poked me, I lost control. My entire body shook as my release ripped through me. Shelly's own release came causing her to writhe and spasm underneath me. Spots were dancing in and out of my field of vision as I waited to catch my breath. Shelly said something, and I eased out of her and collapsed onto the mattress. Then she tucked herself into my side and threw one leg over me.

I draped an arm over her shoulders and squeezed.

We fell asleep not long after.

In the morning, we couldn't stop giggling and kissing as we looked for our clothes. When we were dressed, my skin was still buzzing, and I was still shaking with need. Before she left, I took her again, pressed against the door, with the bottom half of her clothes off. Shelly was even more eager and passionate the second time and kept meeting each thrust with one of her own.

During the wedding, we kept sneaking glances at each other and smiling, basking in the knowledge of our dirty little secret.

As the years went by, our sex life only improved and twenty-five years after the first time we slept together, I still thought she was the most beautiful woman in the world.

Being with her still made me hot and heavy, and it always made me feel like that eager and insatiable young man.

Chapter 7

Cayden

By Cayden Deihl

"I heard it's some pretty hardcore stuff." I rolled the pill between my fingers and paused to sniff it. "You sure this is legit?"

Will snorted and folded his arms over his chest. "Of course, I'm sure. I got it from a guy who got it from his guy. It's legit."

I sniffed it again and paused. "Okay."

Will stood up and rolled his eyes. "You going to quit being a pussy and take it, or what?"

I scowled and rose to my feet. "Let's wait for everyone else to get here."

Especially because I knew Simone was going to kill me if I started without her. She was finishing up some work at the library before our big New Year's Eve party. Will and I had spent the past few hours hanging up streamers and setting out all kinds of refreshments. Renee and Jill were already rifling through the CDs and arguing about the music for the night. Henry was on the balcony, his face half-lit up by the red and orange embers of his cigarette. Out of the corner of my eye, I saw a flash of movement, and Jill slid the door shut and joined him outside.

Seconds later, he had his hands on her ass, and she was draped all over him.

I chuckled and turned away from them. "Someone is getting started early tonight."

I didn't give a shit what the two of them did as long as Simone got here soon.

Because my cock was already twitching and eager for her.

Having her wake up to my head between her legs wasn't enough and neither was getting home after my last class and finding Simon buck naked and waiting for me on the couch. Each day when I got home, she already had her fingers between her legs and was fingering herself. And each day, I dropped my book bag by the door and rushed over to her, already rock hard at the sight of her drenched pussy.

Fuck.

I couldn't get enough of her.

Our weekends weren't any different, with the exception of staying out all night, dancing and drinking until we could barely see straight. Each night when we went home, Simone and I ended up going at it like a bunch of wild rabbits, on the kitchen counter, against the front door, and on every surface of our apartment till we ended up on the bed, tangled up in each other. I took another sip of my beer and felt it trickle down my throat.

Simone arrived a short while later, her cheeks flushed with color, scarf thrown haphazardly over her nape, and flecks of snow clinging to her skirt. She left her bag by the door and called out to everyone. When she made a beeline for me, she took the beer bottle out of my hands and took a long swig. Then she took my hand in hers and led me to the back of Will's apartment. In the storage closet, she pushed me up against the wall and kissed me, tasting like cherry-flavored lip gloss.

I kneaded her ass and bit down on her bottom lip. "What took you so long?"

Simone hoisted herself up and wrapped her legs around my waist. "I had stuff to do."

I rubbed her breasts and stopped inches away from her lips. "The only important thing you have to do tonight is me."

Simone moaned and threw her head back. "Fuck. Do you have any idea how badly I want you right now?"

I thrust against her middle. "Can't you feel how hard you make me?"

Simone ground against me, and her breath hitched in her throat when I lifted her shirt up and squeezed her breasts together. "Everyone else is busy. We've got time."

Simone's answering laugh was breathy and impatient. "I want to."

I placed a hand on her center. "I know you do. I can smell how much you want me."

And it was driving me wild.

I didn't understand why we weren't already fucking each other's brains out.

It wasn't like we hadn't done it in Will's storage room before, or other areas of his apartment. So long as he didn't have to see us, Will didn't care, and neither did we. I moved to flick open the button of her jeans, but Simone stopped me. I unhooked her bra and took one nipple between my teeth. Simone's hand ducked underneath the waistband of my boxers, and she squeezed.

I growled and went back to her button. "What are you waiting for?"

"Tonight isn't about us," Simon said in a husky voice. "Tonight is about the party."

I pressed kisses over her neck. "What does one have to do with the other?"

More importantly, why wasn't I balls deep in her already?

I could smell how much she wanted me.

Simone unhooked her legs and set her feet down. "We should go back outside."

She inched away from me, and I pressed myself against her back. Through the thin fabric of her skirt, I rubbed myself against her. Simone moaned and leaned into my touch. I pressed both of her breasts together and sank my teeth into her neck. She threw her head back and twisted her arm behind her to grip me again. Suddenly, she was hiking up her skirt and panting. Her panties were halfway around her knees when I gripped her hips and positioned myself at her entrance.

I was about to thrust when I heard them call out to us.

Will's voice drifted closer, and he banged on the door a few seconds later. "The two of you can screw each other later. It's New Year's Eve."

I scowled. "Fuck off, Will."

Will banged again, louder this time. "No, come on. It's the Y2K party, for fuck's sake. You don't want to miss it."

Simone sighed and straightened her back. She adjusted her skirt and spun around to face me. I pressed her against the wall and kissed her long and hard, leaving her lips red. Even in the semi-darkness, I didn't miss the smile she gave me, or the extra sway of her hips as she shifted to open the door. I turned my back on the blinding white light and tucked myself back into my jeans. A few moments later, when I was sure I had it under control, I followed Simone outside.

She tucked herself into my side, and we sauntered out of the hallway.

Renee was sitting on Will's lap on the couch, the two of them sharing a bottle of beer. Jill sat on Henry's lap while he played with her hair. I smiled, took a seat on the other side of the couch, and pulled Simone down onto my lap, right over my raging hard-on. She wriggled and tried to get up, but I wouldn't let her. Eventually, when Will pulled out the X pills and passed them out, we all laughed and washed them down with some beer.

It didn't take long for my head to feel light and airy.

I was fondling Simone and trying to think of an excuse to drag her back into the storage closet when she jumped to her feet. Her eyes darted around the room, and she placed her hands on her hips. "Come on, let's play spin the bottle."

A cheer rose through the crowd.

Reene was giggling as Will pulled her into the kitchen in search of a bottle. On the way back, they stopped to kiss, and I could practically see her tongue halfway down his throat. Simone was the one who brought them back to the present with a wave and a cheer. Henry and Jill were quiet as she sat down in between his legs, a look of fierce concentration etched onto her face. I was grinning from ear-to-ear when Simone pulled me onto the carpet and leaned against my side.

I was the first to spin the bottle, and I raised an eyebrow when it landed on Jill.

Simone cheered and clapped. "Alright, you two. Pucker up."

Jill shrugged and leaned forward. "I hope you use mints, Cayden."

I laughed and covered the distance between us. "Don't worry. You'll enjoy this."

Her lips tasted like honey, and it felt like I was floating on clouds. She shifted, and I cupped the back of her neck. Jill made a low noise in the back of her throat, and it sent a jolt through me. When she drifted closer, the smell of her lavender bodywash sent another jolt of desire right through me. Once we drew back, my head was still spinning, and I had my hands clenched into fists.

Simone was smiling as she reached for the bottle to spin it.

It landed on Reene and I.

Neither of us said anything as we closed the gap and kissed.

Kissing Renee was different, like something low and urgent was blossoming within me, and I needed to chase it. I hadn't realized how hard I was cupping the back of her neck, or how tightly she was pressed against me until Simone's voice broke through the haze. I was trying to remember how to breathe when Simone climbed onto my lap and rubbed herself against me. I moved to deepen the kiss, and I groped her through her shirt. Then Simone climbed off my lap and gestured to Jill. Jill crawled over to me, and I could see her hard nipples poking through her shirt.

Simone pulled Henry in for a kiss as Jill rubbed me through my jeans.

I threw my head back and groaned.

Reene and Will were pawing at each other in the background.

Everything floated in and out of focus as Jill touched me, and I watched Simone get groped by Henry. He had one hand between her legs, and the other was pushing her breasts together. Simon's mouth was half open, and she was smiling. Then she removed his hand and glanced over her shoulders at Jill, then her gaze flicked over to Renee. Slowly, Renee stopped and crawled over to me, switching places with Jill.

When Jill and Simone sat in front of each other, Henry and Will drifted closer.

Renee unzipped my jeans, and her hand slid past the waistband of my boxers. I moaned at her expert touch, but I couldn't wrench my gaze away. Simone was fondling Jill, and Jill was pressing kisses against Simone's neck. When Jill found her way to Simone's mouth, Henry and Will began to touch themselves. I licked my dry lips and watched as my girlfriend and Jill made out.

It felt like I was in the middle of a porno.

Now and again, everyone glanced around at everyone else, but no one seemed to mind.

The thick haze that had settled around us was potent and thick.

I cocked a finger at Renee, and she drew closer. I rubbed my hands up and down her arms, and she shivered. Then I pushed her head down, so her mouth was on my raging hard cock. While she sucked and licked, Jill lifted Simone's shirt over her head. She took one of Simone's hard nipples between her teeth and sucked.

I jerked against Renee's mouth.

Jill moved onto Simone's other nipple, and Simone wound her fingers through Jill's thick and dark hair. When the two of them stopped, Jill crawled over to Will and swatted his hand away. She lowered herself onto the carpet and took him into her mouth. Renee stopped sucking and gave me a heated look. Then she wandered over to Henry and climbed onto his lap to kiss him. My head was still spinning when Simone came over and started to stroke me.

When I blinked and glanced down, Jill and Simone were sucking on my cock at the same time. I had my back pressed against the couch, and one hand on the back of each of their heads. My hips kept thrusting, and the two women kept licking and sucking, making low whimpering sounds as they did. Out of the corner of my eye, I saw Renee with her legs stretched out in front of her, completely naked, as Henry stroked her from the back and licked her neck while Will knelt in front of her, sucking on her nipples.

I groaned and threw my head back. "Fuck me. What is in those pills?"

Simone stopped sucking my cock and rose to kiss me. "Only the best, baby. Aren't you enjoying yourself?"

I gripped the back of her neck to keep her in place. "This is the fucking best, baby."

Simone gave me another kiss and wriggled out of my grasp.

When I was about to come, Simone and Jill stopped. The two of them shared another searing kiss during which Simone fingered Jill. I stroked myself as Simone finger fucked her, harder and harder until Jill's entire body writhed and shook. Her head fell into the crook of Simone's neck, and she heaved a deep breath. Jill smiled and pushed Simone back. When Simone was flat on her back, Jill settled in between her legs and began to lick her soaking wet pussy.

I jerked and warmth seeped between my fingers as I came.

When I blinked, Reene was beckoning me forward. She was on her back on the carpet, with her legs spread open and two fingers pushed in between her wet folds. After offering her a slow smile, I bent down to taste her. I sank my nails into her waist, and Renee gripped the back of my head, drawing me closer. I swiped my tongue back and forth over her wet folds, licking and sucking as my heart pounded in my ears.

Suddenly, Renee was shaking and crying out incoherently.

I stopped, crawled up to kiss her, and shifted away with a pant. Henry took my place between her legs, and he played with her nipples while his tongue drove her wild. Renee was still riding out her second high when Will settled in between her legs and dove his tongue in between her wet folds. The two of them were loud and jerking against each other when Jill found me again, furiously stroking myself.

She led me to the couch and pushed me against it.

Jill knelt down in front of me and touched herself. "You have no idea how hot I think you are."

I leaned forward to touch her. "So are you."

Jill licked her lips. "You're so big, too. I bet I can take all of you in my mouth."

Without waiting for a response, she knelt in front of me and took me into her mouth. She licked slowly at first, running her tongue down the sides of my shaft. Then she began to move her mouth back and forth, prompting me to throw my head back and moan. When Jill's movements shifted, and I sensed a little more urgency, my eyes flew open. Henry stood behind

Jill, rubbing himself against her. He slapped her ass and then positioned himself behind her.

Jill stilled when he thrust into her.

I thrust upward and into her mouth. "Too much?"

Jill's eyes rolled into the back of her head. She blew out a breath and shook her head. Over her shoulders, I saw Simone riding Will, who was thrusting upward and grunting. Meanwhile, Renee was next to them on the couch, touching herself and playing with Simone's breasts. Simone ground against Will and placed a hand between Renee's thighs.

I grunted and thrust further into Jill's mouth.

She made a low choking sound, but didn't stop, even when Henry began to pound harder, his skin slapping against hers. Abruptly, I massaged the back of Jill's skull and stopped thrusting. With a smile, I shifted, and Jill fell face forward onto the couch. Henry was still gripping her ass and fucking her hard when I moved away.

Reene found me on the couch and guided me into her.

We were rocking back and forth against each other when she came, her entire body coming undone around my pulsing dick. Will pulled her away shortly after, and Simone appeared in my field of vision, panting and her cheeks flush with pleasure. She placed a hand on my chest and pushed me, so I was flat on my back and staring up at the ceiling. After some kissing and fondling, Simone crawled up, so her pussy was on my face.

I gripped her hips and moaned. "You're so fucking sexy."

She bounced up and down while my tongue darted in and out of her. "Don't stop, Cayden. Don't you ever stop?"

I focused on how she felt on my face, how her juices tasted on my tongue. Then I felt another pair of hands on the lower half of my body. Suddenly, a pair of hands wrapped around my cock, and I twitched. My vision was hazy and unclear as she climbed onto me and guided me into her. I had no idea who was fucking me while I ate out Simone.

But I didn't care.

Not when it felt this good to be wild.

To feel like we didn't have a care in the world.

Simone came with a violent lurch, her body tilting forward as it did. Slowly, she climbed off of me, and I blinked, but my vision still wouldn't clear. Whoever I was fucking was riding me hard and panting heavily the entire time. She whispered my name a few times, and I tried to identify the voice. Then I was coming again, jerking violently as I squeezed my eyes shut. Her release came, and she shook and writhed on top of me. Once I could breathe again, I realized I was flat on my back staring up at the ceiling with my hands curled into fists at my side.

Simone curled up against me, her blonde hair draped over my chest. "It's past midnight."

I kissed her cheek, feeling fulfilled and happily spent. "Happy New Year."

Chapter 8

DeShaun

By DeShaun Wills

I raised an eyebrow and blew smoke out my mouth. After a brief pause, I clicked on the ad and skimmed through the title, realizing that the man in question, a white man with a receding hairline, was in search of a black man to bang his wife.

And all he wanted to do was watch.

After blowing out another puff of smoke, I went to the contact section and drafted up an email. I was in the kitchen filling up a glass of water and looking for something to eat when my laptop pinged. When I went back to the counter, I saw that the man had responded to my email enthusiastically. Smiling, I sent out another email, and his response came a few minutes later.

I was in the middle of my chicken salad sandwich when he sent me an email with a picture attachment. The picture showed a pale white man with receding hair and a small smile on his face. Next to him was a woman with shoulder-length blonde hair, pearly white teeth, and the biggest tits I had ever seen. Shifting from one foot to the other, I leaned forward and zoomed in on the woman.

She had blue eyes, and a sparkle that I recognized.

When I zoomed back out and scrolled down, I realized just how tight her top was. It was practically painted onto her skin and left very little to the imagination, and so was the short skirt she wore, showing off her long slender legs. After staring at her for a while longer, I zoomed back out and studied her husband.

She was fucking gorgeous; the stuff of wet dreams.

He, on the other hand, looked like an everyday kind of Joe, the kind who didn't know how to satisfy a woman like her. Cheryl Kramer looked like she knew how to take it and wanted it rough and dirty. Her husband, Murray, looked like he had seen better days. With a smirk, I leaned back in my chair and touched myself.

I wanted to fuck her, but I was the kind of man who didn't like drama.

Of any kind.

What kind of man would want someone to fuck his wife—especially a woman who looked like a twenty-five-year-old Pamela Anderson, no less?

Shrugging, I sent out another email and drummed my fingers against the desk.

A few minutes later, Cherly's number flashed across the screen, and I snatched the phone off the table. "Hello?"

"Hello? Is this DeShaun?"

"Speaking." I stood up and shoved a hand into the pocket of my jeans. "It's good to hear from you, Cheryl."

"Thank you for getting back to my husband so quickly," Cheryl replied, after a brief pause. "We weren't sure an ad was going to work."

I stepped out onto the balcony and lit up another cigarette. "I was surprised to see the ad."

And even more surprised that they were both so willing.

"I love my husband," Cherly said in a whisper-soft voice. "And he does try in bed...he really does, but I need something...different."

"You need someone who can fuck you properly." I lit up my cigarette and exhaled. "And you're sure he doesn't mind?"

"He likes watching me get fucked by other men," Cherly replied in the same soft voice. "Even more if it's a black man."

I blew out another breath of smoke. "I have a few conditions if I agree to this."

"Of course."

"Is Murray next to you?"

Cheryl's voice drifted off and turned muffled. Then the two of them came back on, and I heard an echo in the background. "What are your conditions?"

"I don't want to be touched except by Cheryl."

"Understood," Murray responded, a little too eagerly. "I have no interest in you, DeShaun. I just want someone who can please my wife."

"No jerking off while I bang your wife," I added after a brief pause. "It's better if you're fully dressed."

Because the thought of his dick was a major turn-off.

And if I was expected to give the blonde bombshell the fuck of a lifetime then I needed to be able to focus on her and only her. Having her husband touch his limp dick and pleasure himself wasn't on the list of things I wanted to see or even imagine.

"That's also fine," Murray said cheerfully. "I just like watching, DeShaun, and I want you to fuck her any way you want. As if I'm not watching."

"And you can be as dirty as you want," Cheryl added in the background. "We want you to enjoy yourself, too."

I nodded. "Good. When do you want to get together?"

"Is Friday too soon?"

"Tomorrow? I have a shift till six, but it should be fine. I'll shower and then—"

"Don't shower," Cheryl interrupted breathlessly. "I like a little sweat and dirt."

I smiled as my cock twitched in my pants. "Okay, good. Send me your address then, and I'll see you when I get there."

After I hung up, my phone buzzed to indicate an incoming text. I fished it out of my pocket and studied the address through a thin plume of smoke. Smiling, I stubbed out my cigarette and went back inside to look at Cheryl's picture. Then I took the laptop inside and set it down on the nightstand. I touched myself while looking at her picture. Using one hand, I stroked myself while the other zoomed in on her picture. My gaze drifted from her mouth to her tits as I imagined what they would feel like.

Her full sensuous lips would feel good against my skin.

And I already knew she was going to feel good when I was balls deep inside of her, her wet juices all over my dick. Groaning, I squeezed my eyes shut, and it wasn't long before cum filled my hands, some of it dripping onto my bed sheet. As soon as I finished, I stood up and went to the bathroom to wash my hands. Then I stripped my bed and threw the sheet into the laundry hamper. After unfolding a new sheet set, I took my laptop outside and twisted the screen, so she was looking at me while I cooked.

In the morning, I was already hard for her.

By the time afternoon rolled around, I was trying to focus on my work and not think of what was waiting for me. Five in the afternoon came, and I was growing impatient. Five minutes to six, I was racing to clock myself out. I got into the car, yanked the door shut, and turned the key in the ignition. I tapped my fingers along to the music and followed the instructions on my phone. I pulled up to a house in the suburbs located just outside the city, where hundreds of two-story houses were on either side of me, with lush green lawns and fancy cars in the driveways.

Cheryl and Murray were waiting for me in the doorway, smiling from ear-to-ear.

I killed the ignition, pushed the door open, and got out. When I slammed the door shut, Cheryl's smile grew wider, and she stepped out from behind her husband. She was taller than he was, but she still folded against me when I reached for her, smelling like peaches and expensive perfume. Murray and I shook hands as he ushered me inside.

After a round of drinks, I saw Cheryl loosen up and unbutton the first few buttons on her shirt. Murray pressed a kiss to her cheek and leaned back against his stool. Smiling, I polished off the rest of my drink and stood up. Cheryl was staring at me as I pulled my shirt over my head, revealing my toned and sweaty stomach.

She licked her red lips and blushed. "You're in very good shape."

"You'll find out just how much in a bit," I said in a husky voice. With a smirk, I crossed over to her and pulled her into my arms. Cheryl tilted her head back to look up at me, and I could smell her arousal. I tilted her chin up and kissed her.

She kissed me back with a hunger and yearning that surprised me.

Her hands went from my shoulders, glided down my back, and stopped at my ass. She gave it a firm squeeze and smiled into the kiss. I hoisted her up and carried her over to the counter. After setting her down, I stepped in between her legs and rubbed myself against her. Cheryl undid the rest of the buttons on her shirt, revealing the creamy white skin underneath. She threw her head back and undid the clasp on her bra.

When her breasts spilled forward, I took one between my teeth and sucked.

Murray sat a few feet away, watching us intently while he leisurely sipped on his beer. I moved onto the other breast and cast a quick glance in his direction. He was clearly turned on by the sight, but as per our agreement, he didn't do anything. Once her nipples were hard, I rubbed Cheryl over her panties.

She was already soaking wet.

I snuck one finger under the waistband of her underwear and growled. "How long have you been holding yourself back?"

"Too long." Cheryl moaned and bucked against my touch. I inserted another finger and used my free hand to grip the back of her neck. "God, that feels good."

I swiped my hands back and forth, slowly at first, then harder and harder.

Cheryl came with a violent shake, but I didn't wait for her to exhale before I carried her upstairs. Murray was hot on our heels, and he sat down on the couch in their bedroom. After setting Cheryl down on the bed, I peeled off my jeans and boxers. Her eyes widened as she took in the length and size of me, and her mouth parted.

Cheryl's hands trembled as she took off her skirt and panties.

She threw them into a heap on the floor and reached for me.

Our bodies collided, and I kissed her again, hard enough to make her pant my name. She linked her feet over my torso as I positioned myself at her entrance and circled my hips. Cheryl kept trying to draw me closer, but I wanted to drag this out. She was already wet, but I wanted her to be desperate. I wanted her unable to think of anyone or anything else.

Except for me.

Only me.

Her blonde hair fell forward, and her boobs bounced up and down as she ground against me. With a growl, I thrust into her and waited. Once I filled her to the hilt, I eased out and slammed back into her again. She cried out and raked her fingers over my back, marking me with her nails. Eventually, I threw her legs up over my shoulders and pushed myself, so I was all the way in.

Cheryl didn't falter.

She had an appetite even I hadn't anticipated, and I loved every second of it.

Each dip and creak of the bed, each groan, and each touch was driving me more and more wild. The sound of Murray sipping on his beer in the background only made it better. Cheryl shook and writhed as the force of orgasm ripped through her. I set her feet down and kissed a path down to her inner thighs. Then I slid down, sunk my nails into her waist, and began to lick her pussy.

Whenever I glanced up at her, she was looking at Murray through hooded eyes, her hair a wild mess on top of her face.

I reached between us to play with her breasts, and she fell back against the mattress.

When another orgasm ripped through her, Cheryl was sweaty and panting. I helped her sit up and spun her around, so she was facing her husband. Then I pushed her forward, so she was on her hands and knees in front of him. I placed a hand on her back and slammed into her.

Cheryl looked directly at her husband and exhaled. "I forgot what a big cock feels like."

I eased out of her and thrust back in. Then I reached between us and played with her nipples. She was panting and moaning and bucking wildly against me. "You could never fuck me like this fucking bull stud can."

I thrust harder, enjoying the feel of my skin slapping against hers. Cheryl moaned even louder, her eyes never leaving her husband's face. I wound my fingers through her hair and yanked her neck back, hard. Her breathing grew heavier, but her movements grew even more frantic.

Like she was trying to prove something.

But I didn't give a shit what it was, not as long as she continued to let me fuck her.

Being balls deep in a woman like Cheryl was better than anything I could've imagined.

Her skin was soft; softer than anything I'd ever felt, and even when she was covered in sweat and her juices, she still smelled amazing.

Fucking hell.

I wanted to fuck her every corner of the house until she'd had her fill of me. Then I wanted to take a breather and watch her pleasure herself through a thin plume of smoke. After I was done, I wanted to bend her over and pound into her while she was pressed against a wall, leaving her nowhere to run and nowhere to hide.

It's no wonder her husband couldn't satisfy her.

She was a wild animal, begging to be ravaged and taken like the dirty slut she was.

"You're not even a man compared to DeShaun," Cheryl said, in between pants. She was still looking at her husband, but his face gave nothing away. "How does it feel to know only he can fuck me like this? Only he can pleasure me like this, and all you can do is watch."

I eased out of her and slapped her ass, hard enough to leave a mark.

What the hell was she trying to do by egging him on?

Was Cheryl trying to get me killed?

I waited for a while longer, but when nothing happened and Murray still had the same pleasant look on his face, I growled. "You like my cock more than this old man's?"

Cheryl loosened a breath. "I do."

"You do, what?" I gripped the back of her neck again and pounded into her so hard that I was sure the bed was going to break. "Say it out loud."

"I like your cock more than his." Cheryl moaned and used one hand to prop herself up, and the other to push her breasts together. "You're so big and so... skilled."

"That's not the only thing I am." I released the back of her neck and bucked harder, a strange sort of buzz starting in my veins. I had no idea what it was about knowing that Murray was watching, or how much Cheryl was taunting him that drove me so wild, but it did.

Knowing that he couldn't make her feel this good made me feel powerful.

Invincible even.

Because when she crawled into bed every night, it wasn't her husband she thought of.

I was going to make sure it was me.

When she touched herself, I wanted her to imagine my dick between her wet folds, slamming into her over and over like there was no tomorrow. And I wanted her to picture her legs over her head as I screwed her brains out until she couldn't walk straight.

Because that was the kind of man I was.

"I'm going to fill up your tight little pussy like his little cock never could," I said in a thick voice. "Do you understand me?"

Cheryl moaned in response.

I dug my nails into her hips and stopped thrusting. "What did you say?"

Cheryl whimpered and wriggled. "Why are you stopping?"

"Because I asked you a question." I stroked her ass, slowly at first and then I slapped it again. "I want to hear you say you understand."

Cheryl twisted her head to look at me, and the look on her face almost made me want to bury my cock in between her breasts and come all over her face. "I understand."

I started thrusting again. "Good, because I know you've never had it this good, have you?"

Cheryl's eyes widened. "No."

"What's it feel like to get fucked by a real man, bitch?" I rammed into her so hard she fell face forward onto the mattress. When she was close, I eased out of her and flipped her, so she was on her back facing me. Her face was red, and her eyes were filled with an unfamiliar gleam. I glanced over at Murray, and then I hoisted her legs up over her head. Once I was back inside of her, I moved again, harder and faster than I ever had before.

And she was screaming and panting the whole time.

"That's it," I urged in a thick voice. "Keep taking it. You like to be fucked hard, don't you? Because you're a dirty little slut and no one else does it for you."

Cheryl's hands fell on either side of her, and she grabbed a handful of the sheets. "No one does it for me."

"You like being at my mercy," I continued in the same tone of voice. I laced my fingers through hers and wouldn't release them. "You like knowing that I can keep going, that I can keep fucking you like this, hard and deep."

"Oh...Oh, Deshaun. Oh, God...*mmmmm*. Fuck, yes!"

"Don't come until I tell you to," I warned with a growl. "Because I'm going to come inside your cunt, and you're going to like it."

Cheryl moaned and squeezed her muscles.

A heartbeat later, I exploded, my entire body jerking as it did. Cheryl's release followed soon after, and she shook so hard, that the bed dipped underneath us. I rolled off of her and brought my hand behind my head. Cheryl crawled over to the edge of the bed and beckoned Murray forward. He stood up, knelt in front of her, and cupped the back of her neck.

The two of them kissed like they were the ones who had been fucking.

Then they both turned to me with bright smiles as Murray draped an arm over her shoulders. "That was perfect. Thank you."

Chapter 9

Jim

By Jim Walsh-Dunn

"I'm having a great time, Jim." My wife of six years placed a hand on my arm and smiled at me. "Who would've thought a trip to New York would be exactly what we needed?"

I smiled and laced my fingers through hers. "Even the long line to the Empire State Building?"

"Worth it." Janine smiled and used her free hand to take a sip of her drink. "And I loved going to see the statue of liberty."

I squeezed her fingers. "Good. I'm glad."

Because we'd both been working so hard lately, and I thought we deserved a little pick-me-up. Driving down to New York for the weekend was proving to be one of my better ideas, especially since we'd spent most of yesterday walking around, taking in the sights and drinking like there was no tomorrow.

I was on my second rum and coke of the day, and I had no intention of stopping anytime soon. There were few other people at the bar as the sun dipped below the horizon and soft music played in the background. With a smile, I sat up straighter and pulled Janine closer. Her eyes were glazed over, and she was looking gorgeous in her knee-length dress and open-toed sandals. When she wrapped her arms around my neck and kissed me, it felt like I was floating on a cloud.

I was on a high, and I didn't want to come down anytime soon.

Janine inched closer on her stool and pressed herself against me. When I gripped the back of her neck, she nibbled on my lower lip, and I exhaled. Her tongue darted in and moved around my mouth, making my head spin. With a smile, I tugged her forward and pulled her onto my lap. Janine gasped when I rubbed myself against her.

She threw her head back and giggled. "People are going to start looking."

"I don't care." I continued to rub myself against her, my blood turning molten. "Let's get out of here."

Janine squirmed and stood up. "Not yet. I have an idea."

I raised an eyebrow. "Oh?"

"I saw a sex store nearby, and I thought we could do a little Secret Santa," Janine said, the words pouring out of her in a rush. "I thought I would go first and buy you a gift. Then you can go and buy me a toy, and we both have to use it on each other."

I grinned. "I like the way you think."

Janine smiled and leaned forward to kiss me. "I'll be right back."

With that, she took a last sip of her martini and darted off. On her way past, she danced out of my reach and skipped out of the bar. A few people twisted to face her, but no one said anything. I eyed her over the rim of my glass and watched as she pushed the swinging doors of the hotel open. Once she was outside, she glanced down both sides of the street and then straightened her back. I kept my gaze on her as I signaled for another drink.

Janine was practically sprinting into the shop.

I was on my fifth rum and coke and feeling a pleasant buzz pump through my veins when Janine came back through the double doors. She had a large plastic bag in her hand, and her cheeks were flushed with color. Her shoes were in her hand and she was smiling so broadly that I couldn't help but smile in return. Giggling, Janine slid into the seat opposite me and placed the bag in her lap.

I polished off my drink and stood up. "I guess it's my turn."

"Buy whatever you want, and we can meet back in the room in half an hour." Janine leaned forward and flagged the bartender down. "I can't wait to see what you get."

I kissed her cheek. "Me either."

With a spring in my step, I stepped through the revolving doors. Outside, I shoved both hands into my pockets and enjoyed the warmth of the sun on my back. People rushed past me in either direction as I made a beeline for the sex store. While I waited for the light to turn red, I imagined what kind of selection they had. By the time the light turned, and a surge of people stepped forward, I was no closer to figuring out what I wanted.

The store smelled liked candy and perfume.

It had rows and rows of sex toys, all proudly on display and under bright fluorescent lighting. A few uninterested-looking men and women standing behind counters. I perused the rows of edible underwear, whips, and furry handcuffs. Then I stopped in front of the vibrators and studied them. Out of the corner of my eye, I saw a flash of movement; a man was reaching for a strap-on cock. With a tilt of my head, I approached the display, a wide array of shapes and sizes, and paused.

Before I could talk myself out of it, I chose a decent-sized peg and carried it to the cashier.

The red-haired woman with a nose piercing and a bored look rang me up. After paying, and her handing them over, the woman handed me a plastic bag similar to Janine's. I was smiling and humming to myself as I walked out and lingered on the sidewalk.

After checking my watch, I headed back to the hotel.

I cast a quick glance in the direction of the bar, but wasn't surprised not to find Janine. I shifted the bag from one hand to the other and made a beeline for the elevator. There, I tapped my foot impatiently and waited for the familiar ping. The doors slid open, revealing a carpeted blue-colored hallway with land-scape paintings on either side of the walls. Outside our door, I patted my pocket for my key card.

The door clicked open, and Janine's voice called out to me.

She had the lights dimmed and a few candles lit, casting long shadows across the walls. When I stepped in and kicked the door shut, Janine stepped forward in a lacy red nightgown, with her hair piled on top of her head. Wordlessly, she pulled me to her and kissed me soundly.

"What did you get?"

I pulled out the strap-on cock and cleared my throat. "I thought we could try something different."

Janine glanced from the strap-on peg to my face, her lips twitching. "Really?"

I nodded.

Janine threw her head back and began to laugh. "Well, I feel silly."

She darted deeper into the room and came back with her bag. When she pulled out her own strap-on cock, she was still laughing. "I guess we both had the same thought. You've been hinting for a while, so I thought I'd surprise you."

I smiled. "I was trying to be subtle."

Janine giggled. "No, you weren't, but it's okay. This trip is all about trying new things."

I crossed over to her and took her into my arms. "I love you. Have I said that lately?"

"I love you, too." Janine lifted her head, and her lips found mine. For a while, we stood there kissing while I rubbed my hands up and down her arms. She shivered and ran her hands along my back, stopping at my ass. After patting it, one hand drifted back up to my shoulders, and the other darted between us.

She untucked my shirt, and her fingers began to stroke my skin.

I smiled into the kiss and bit down on her bottom lip. Her mouth parted, and my tongue darted in, sweeping in a large circle. When Janine's hands lingered on my shirt, I stopped kissing her and drew back. I drew it over my head and tossed it into a heap on the floor. Then I stepped out of my jeans and pulled my boxers down.

Janine's chest was heaving, and I could smell her desire.

I took her hand and led her into the bedroom. There, I pushed her onto the bed and framed her face between my hands. Janine ran her hands up and down my arms as I rubbed myself against her. Slowly, I wrenched my lips away and kissed a path down to her stomach. After gripping her waist, my tongue darted in between her clit. She bucked and writhed against me while my tongue darted and moved around her wet folds. Janine came with a violent lurch, her grip on the back of my neck tightening.

In a daze, she sat up and snatched the strap-on off the nightstand. She secured it around her waist and motioned for me to turn around. Heart hammering unsteadily, I gave her my back and propped myself up on all fours. Janine lined up behind me, placed her hands on either side of my hips, and rubbed my behind.

"Slowly," I instructed in a thick voice. "You'll know when to go faster."

Janine used her fingers first, and I groaned to signal my satisfaction. She used another finger to explore, and I leaned into her touch. When she paused, I heard a squeezing sound and glanced over my shoulders. Smirking, Janine slathered a generous amount of lube onto her fingers and rubbed them together.

Then she slapped my butt with her free hand, and her smirk grew wider. Using her finger, she massaged my hole.

When I started to groan, her finger started moving in and out.

"Hold on." Janine's finger shifted away, and I turned in time to see her throw herself over the mattress and wrench a drawer open. "I heard this helps, too."

I raised an eyebrow. "Is that a butt plug?"

Janine nodded and grinned. "I've done my homework."

"I can see that." My pulse quickened, and my heart missed a beat as Janine held the butt plug up and crawled over to me. I watched with bated breath as she positioned it behind my rectum and sat up straighter. Her breasts were spilling out of her nightgown, and she was licking her lips. I glanced from the plug to her face and thought I was going to come then and there.

Janine held my gaze as she pushed the plug in, slowly, languidly, as if we had all of the time in the world. Then she held onto the safety chord and used her other hand to move the plug around. Wave after wave of pleasure began to build within me. It was rubbing me in all of the right places, and it felt better than anything I could've imagined.

There was something intense and vulnerable about Janine standing behind me while finger fucking my asshole.

Something primal and sensual and dirty.

It spoke to something deep within me that made me start to rock back and forth, wanting to take the plug in as deeply as possible. Janine pressed a kiss to my lower back and squeezed my ass, hard. When I wanted more, I glanced back over my shoulders at Janine and gave her a small imperceptible nod. She removed the plug, wiped it down, and placed it on the nightstand. With trembling fingers, she strapped on the dildo and sat on her legs.

"I've always wanted to know what it would feel like to have this much power," Janine whispered into my back. "I like that you're not afraid to be dominated by me."

I shook my head, thin beads of sweat erupting on my forehead. "I want to be dominated by you. I want to be completely at your mercy."

Especially if it meant I got to be fucked in the ass.

Janine lined up behind me and gripped my ass with both hands. Her fingers sank into my flesh as she thrust into me. My eyes rolled to the back of my head as I threw my head back and moaned. Janine kept one hand on my ass, and the other glided over my back, stroking my already sensitive skin. I ground against her, and she made a low surprised noise in her throat.

"Didn't expect that, did you?"

Janine chuckled, eased out, and slammed back into me. "I can tie you up if that's how you want to play. Have you been a bad boy, Jim?"

I swallowed and nodded, a little too quickly. "Yes. I've been very bad. I should be punished."

Janine eased back out and thrust further into me, sending little pinpricks of desire racing through every part of me. "How badly do you want me to punish you?"

I braced myself on my elbows, my mind racing. "As hard as you can."

Janine leaned back and tapped my back. When I spun around, she gestured to the headboard, and I smirked. "I had no idea you had such a wild streak."

Once my forehead was pressed against the headboard, and I was on all fours again, Janine gave me what I wanted. She lifted one hand over my head and pinned it against my back. With a growl, Janine began to thrust in and out of me. I used my other hand to try and keep myself propped up, but it was all so new.

So overwhelming.

All I could think about was how much more I wanted, how much more I needed.

What else didn't I know about Janine, and how far she was willing to take this?

I squeezed my eyes shut and focused on how it felt to have her fingers on my bare skin, stroking and pinching. Then I switched my focus to the feeling of her easing in and out of me in slow and practiced strokes, like we'd been doing this forever. The longer she thrust in and out of my ass, the less awkward it felt.

Janine was enjoying herself more than I thought she would as she highlighted, in graphic detail, all of the ways she wanted to violate me.

To make me beg for her to take me.

It was turning me on even more.

Sweating and pulse thumping erratically against my chest, I reached between my legs and began to stroke myself. I pumped slowly at first, building momentum with each stroke, then went faster. Eventually, Janine released my other hand, and her hand darted between us. She took my dick between her hands and squeezed.

Having her fuck me in the ass while pumping me was almost more than I could take.

But I braced my arms on either side of the headboard and ground into her touch, into her hands, and her hips. She responded by thrusting harder, as if her life depended on it.

"How does it feel?"

I glanced at her over my shoulders. "It feels good."

"Just good?" Janine glanced up and held my gaze. "I'm going to need a little more than that if we're going to keep having fun like this, Jim."

"It feels amazing. You know what would be even better?"

Janine shook her head.

"Play with yourself. I want to watch you pleasure yourself," I said in a thick voice. Janine moaned and dropped one finger between the strap-on and her soaking cunt. She stroked herself while continuing to pump me. Her other hand came up to press her tits together, and my heart began to pound in my ears.

Was this how it felt like to be in her shoes?

To be so thoroughly and completely branded and claimed?

Janine was making little whimpering noises that were like music to my ears. I didn't even care that everyone on our floor could probably hear us, or that they were probably wondering why we were so into it. All I cared about was that Janine didn't stop or falter.

She wanted this as much as I did.

When the waves of pleasure grew stronger; strong enough to overtake me, I stopped bucking and twisted to face her. Janine was panting and sweating and red faced. I shifted, so she fell backward and gave me a confused look. With a smirk, I climbed on top of Janine and kissed her soundly. After removing the dildo, I threw her legs over my shoulders and thrust into her. She cried out and raked her fingers over my back.

Janine sank her nails into my shoulders and lifted her head. "I want you to cum inside of me."

I held her arms on either side of her and groaned. "That's exactly what I plan on doing."

She made another low whimpering sound and bucked against me. I eased in and out of her, slowly at first, then faster and harder. Janine tried to link her feet over my neck, but I wouldn't let her. Because after watching her take the reins, I liked being back on top.

And in control.

When I finally let Janine link her legs around my waist, she groaned. I buried my face in her neck and exhaled. The sweet smell of her washed over me as I parted my mouth and sank my teeth into her flesh. She tossed her head to the side and hissed. I slammed back into her and circled my hips, enjoying how it felt to lose myself in between her wet folds.

Abruptly, I sat up, pulled Janine against me, and continued to thrust.

Her breathing quickened, and her rhythm changed, turning wild and reckless. We rocked back and forth against each other, the bed dipping and creaking with each movement. Eventually, Janine took my bottom lip between her teeth and tugged. I lowered my head to take one nipple in between my teeth and tugged.

She threw her head back, and her entire body shook.

Janine's release was violent, and it made the whole bed shake. When she was done, I gave a few more quick thrusts and came deep inside of her while she was still chanting my name.

Chapter 10

Peter

By Peter Pullman

"You're in such good shape for a personal trainer." Kelly ran her long-manicured nails down my chest and paused at the waistband of my jeans. "Were you this disciplined when you were an athlete?"

I lifted my drink to my lips. "I was a lot more disciplined."

Kelly raised an eyebrow and reached for her own drink. "Is that so?"

"Why do you think they call me the best?"

Athletes clambered for my attention, and when they came flocking, so did the women. Tall ones, short ones, skinny and curvy, and everything in between. I had spent the past few years building up a reputation for myself as the trainer to beat.

And the man every woman wanted to fuck.

When I was forced to retire in my early twenties, media outlets predicted I would become another washed-up white male athlete. Now, here I was almost thirty years later and still proving them wrong. At fifty, I was in the best shape of my life and showing no signs of stopping. As I glanced at Kelly over the rim, I kept seeing images of the night we had together.

I saw Kelly with her legs over my shoulders as I slammed into her.

Then I saw her on her hands and knees, with my cock in her mouth as her full and luscious lips sucked and didn't stop. When she leaned in closer, offering me ample view of her cleavage, I saw her riding my cock while my fingers darted in and out of her pussy.

Kelly ran in some of the circles as I did as a publicist to some of the biggest athletes in the world, but even though I was fifteen years her senior, she had the hunger and ambition of a much older woman.

And the insatiable appetite of a teenager.

It made me get all hot and heavy whenever I was around her.

Even now, hours after our fuck sessions, my cock twitched at the smell and proximity of her. Kelly smirked as if she sensed my train of thought. Then she leaned forward, and I caught another whiff of her. She placed a hand on my thigh, and her mouth was suddenly next to my ear.

"Last night was fun."

I placed a hand on her arm. "It was."

She nibbled on my lower lip, her hot breath sending goosebumps all over my skin. "But I heard there's more. When am I going to experience that?"

I leaned back to look at her and paused.

She had been hinting for weeks now, and while I didn't usually hesitate to introduce the women I fucked to my particular brand of fun, Kelly was different.

She was much younger than the women I experimented with.

I had to be sure she was ready.

With a smirk, I reached for my drink. "What makes you think you're ready?"

Kelly moved her mouth back to my ear and exhaled. "Did you see me last night? I was on fire, and I could've kept going if we hadn't been forced to stop. I want more, Peter."

She leaned away from me and went to sit in the booth opposite me. Then she curled her finger around a mug and eyed me over the rim.

I glanced over her shoulders, at the window offering an unobstructed view of the sidewalk, where people raced past in either direction. The afternoon sun was low in the sky, and Kelly and I had been sitting here for the past hour, making small talk over drinks and pastries. Already, I was formulating a way to leave, but her words stopped me dead in my tracks.

Maybe Kelly wasn't so innocent after all.

Underneath the table, I felt her shift and lift her leg up. She ran it down the inside of my thigh, stopped between my legs, and stroked me. The reaction was instant, with my dick springing to attention as if it were at her command. Kelly smiled and continued to stroke me with her foot. When I growled, she only grew bolder and ducked under the booth. Her fingers were on my thighs in no time and fumbling with the zipper of my pants. I angled my body to hide her and was suddenly thankful for the tablecloths obscuring her activity.

If Kelly wanted my help learning how to be an adventurous slut, I was more than happy to oblige. Especially when I felt my zipper come undone, and that her mouth had found its target. I used one hand to grip my drink, and the other gripped the edge of the table, praying Kelly didn't give us away. I bit down on my bottom lip to keep the groan from erupting when her mouth closed around my shaft.

Jesus Christ.

This was a little too easy.

Where the hell did someone like Kelly find the nerve to give me a blowjob in broad daylight, in the middle of a restaurant?

And how in the hell did she get so good at it?

I barely heard her as she moved, even as every inch of me was aware of her. When the waitress came back with a refill, I had to give her a thin smile. As I was about to cum, Kelly stopped and came out from under the table, holding a fork in her hand. She cast a glance around the restaurant, a sheepish smile on her face.

Then she wiped her mouth and gave me a look through lowered lashes.

I had a hard-on that wasn't going away anytime soon.

I drummed my fingers against the desk. "You want to have fun? Alright, let's take you for a test drive."

Without waiting for a response, I whipped out my phone and dialed Lisa's number.

She picked up on the fifth ring, sounding breathless and pleased.

Less than an hour later, Lisa came into the bar and sat down next to Kelly. She played with her hair, stroked her cheeks, and fondled her under the table. After a quick smile in my direction, Lisa stood up and drew Kelly to her feet. I threw Lisa my key on her way past and paused to take some bills out of my wallet. After throwing them on the table, I raced outside to find the two of them a few feet ahead.

Lisa had her arm linked through Kelly's, her hand comfortable resting on Kelly's ass.

Outside my apartment building, Lisa took Kelly into her arms and kissed her, soundly. A few onlookers hooted and hollered. I pressed myself against Kelly and kissed the back of her neck. She moaned and twisted her arm over her head. I caught her by the wrist and pushed her hand forward.

"Not yet. If you want to play our games, you have to play by our rules," I said in a thick voice.

Upstairs, Lisa wasted no time in getting Kelly naked. Lisa draped herself over the bed and fondled Kelly's breasts while I stroked myself. Then I positioned myself behind Kelly and gripped her ass. Her breath hitched in her throat as Lisa shifted under her and took one nipple between her teeth. Kelly stroked Lisa and fingered her while I fucked her from behind.

I thrust in and out of Kelly like I was trying to prove something.

She bucked against me while pleasuring Lisa.

At some point, Lisa took a vibrator out of my nightstand and was using it on herself while Kelly kissed her neck. The two of them were still making out, sensual mouths sucking and biting, and it was one of the hottest things I'd ever seen. I alternated between staring at them and gripping Kelly's ass, treating it like it was the holiest of grails. When Kelly's body shook, a powerful orgasm ripping through her, I sank my nails into her waist. She fell forward onto Lisa's chest and began to lick her nipples.

Lisa's release came shortly after.

I continued to fuck Kelly until I couldn't see straight.

I came with a violent lurch and spilled into Kelly, who twisted to face me. Once my body was done jerking, I eased out of her and collapsed onto the bed. I faced the ceiling while Lisa and Kelly lay down on either side of me purring into my ears and stroking me. After Lisa left, Kelly rode my dick as if she was starved.

Or desperate for something.

I screwed her until she was panting and screaming my name.

Still, it wasn't enough.

A few days later, she was fast asleep in my bed when I placed a mug of coffee under her nose. The steam wafting from the mug woke her up so quickly that she jolted in bed. I placed the mug on the nightstand and pushed her back against the mattress. Kelly was still half asleep as I buried my face in between her legs and sucked on her throbbing wet pussy.

She came with a scream, and I leaned up to kiss her. "You better get some rest. Tonight is a big night."

Kelly curled her fingers around the mug and blinked. "What do you mean?"

"I've invited three of my friends over tonight. Welcome to the big leagues, kid. None of them can wait to fuck you."

Kelly's expression lit up. "All of them?"

"All of them, but I'm going to be the last to cum inside of you and make you scream." I gave her a few quick strokes before I pulled away. "You'd better get ready."

Hours later, after a long shower, a large meal, and a quick nap, Kelly was ready.

She stood by the door in her five-inch heels and a dress with a plunging neckline that brushed the top of her knees. At seven, the doorbell rang and three of my friends came in. Josh, the tall blonde one, immediately pressed Kelly against the nearest wall and started to kiss her. Marcus peeled off his coat, draped it over the back of a chair, and began to rub himself against her side. Liam, on the other hand, stood behind the kitchen counter sipping on his beer.

"Enjoying the show?"

Liam took a quick sip and smirked. "I'll enjoy it better when she's down on her knees."

I unscrewed the cap on my beer and smiled. "I know what you mean."

Josh was kissing Kelly aggressively now, his tongue sliding in and out of her mouth. When he wrenched his lips away, he pressed hot, open-mouthed kisses down the side of her neck while Marcus played with her breasts over her shirt. Then Josh and Marcus switched, so that Marcus was feeling her up while Josh lifted her shirt and sucked on her nipples.

From where I stood, I could already see how turned-on Kelly was.

She was panting and gripping the back of Josh's head while he moved from one nipple to the other, twisting and tugging. Abruptly, Josh released her, and Marcus took her to the couch. He pushed her back, so she sank in between the pillows and was at eye level with his waist. Smirking, Kelly's hands went to the button of his jeans.

She unclipped them and pushed them down, allowing his erection to spring free.

Kelly licked a path down his shift and then back up, making little moaning sounds the entire time. Then she took Marcus inside of her mouth, and he began to thrust. Meanwhile, Josh stood to the side watching them while he stroked himself. Liam stepped out from behind the counter and went over to where Kelly sat.

He sat down next to her and began to stroke her arms, her boobs, and everything in between. Kelly faltered and shot him a look out of the corner of her eye. Liam gave her a wicked smile, but didn't stop. When she stopped to catch her breath, Liam pulled her dress over her head, leaving her completely naked except for the heels. Kelly fell back against the couch, legs behind her head as Marcus thrust in and out of her.

Liam and Josh both hung back and watched and stroked themselves.

It was getting increasingly hard for me to stand there, sipping on my beer and watching her get banged. Still, when she looked over at me, I shifted from one side to the other and smirked. Kelly gave me a knowing look, squeezed her shut, and bucked against Marcus. He leaned forward, so her legs were over his shoulders.

"Fucking hell, bitch." Marcus was breathing heavily now and moving with wild and animal-like abandon. "You sure know how to take it like a slut, don't you?"

Kelly removed her legs and pushed Marcus back, so he sat on the couch. She climbed on top of him, threw one leg up on either side, and ground into him. His fingers went to her waist and dug into the sensitive skin there. She rode him hard, her tits bouncing up and down while I watched, my mouth completely dry. Then she looked directly at me while Marcus threw his head back and groaned.

Marcus was still catching his breath when Kelly stood up and beckoned Josh and Liam over. She pushed Josh onto the couch and climbed on top of him. Then she lifted her hips and lowered herself onto Liam, who immediately began to play with her nipples. He was stroking and flicking them while Kelly rocked back and forth. Liam was pressed against her back, stroking the skin there when he hoisted her hips. Kelly glanced over her shoulders at him and smiled. When Liam entered her from behind, Kelly's moan reverberated throughout the entire apartment.

Together, Liam and Josh fucked her like there was no tomorrow.

Marcus was leaning against the wall, furiously stroking himself by now.

Kelly threw her head back, and Liam gripped the back of her neck. He pressed a kiss there, then sank his teeth into the sensitive flesh. Josh alternated between sucking and biting on her nipples, and despite how intense it must've felt Kelly showed no signs of stopping. She was squeezing both of them for every last bit of pleasure they were worth.

And neither of them minded a bit.

On the contrary, if their grunts and moans were anything to be, they were enjoying themselves as much as Kelly was. Eventually, Josh thrusted upward, and his entire body shook. Once it did, Kelly stopped riding him, and he moved out from under her. Liam gripped her hips and thrust with a frenzied rhythm. With a smirk, Marcus walked over to them and knelt on the couch. Kelly stroked his thighs and then took him in her mouth.

He rocked back and forth as he thrust in and out of her mouth.

Liam ran his hands along her back and gave her ass a firm slap. "Marcus was right. You really can't get enough, can you?"

Kelly made a low noise in the back of her throat.

"You're a fucking beast, and you need all four of us to fuck you otherwise you won't feel satisfied." Liam's thrusts changed, turning wilder and more frantic. Marcus came again, this time inside of Kelly's mouth.

She swallowed and glanced over her shoulders at Liam. His expression was dark and full of hunger as he continued to ram into her. Then Kelly lost her balance and fell face forward against the mattress. Liam pinned her arms on either side of her while she muttered his name.

Liam's thrusts stopped abruptly as his entire body jerked.

Kelly lifted her head and sat up to kiss him.

Marcus and Josh were fondling each other and groaning. She walked right past them and made a beeline for me. I set down my beer as Kelly kissed me. My lips were tingling, and the blood was roaring in my ears as she helped me out of my clothes. Her fingers were quick and deft as they moved over my flushed skin. She pulled me to the couch and pushed me onto it. We started kissing, harder this time, all tongue and teeth, a strange yearning building inside of me.

Holy shit.

This woman was an absolute man-eater.

And I didn't give a shit, so long as I got to bang her brains out.

I wanted to be the one to leave her in a heap on the floor.

I kissed a path from her neck down to her thighs and pushed her legs open. Kelly threw her head back and played with her nipples while she watched me. Using one finger, I stroked her center. Then I pushed one finger in, then another. Once Kelly was bucking against me, I replaced my fingers with my tongue. She was so wet that it made my eyes roll to the back of my head.

Kelly was crying out my name while I drove my tongue in and out of her.

Then Liam stepped into view and rubbed his dick over her face. She smiled, lifted her hand, and gripped him. Liam's eyes were bulging out of his sockets when she led him into her mouth. Her full and sensuous lips moved up and down his shaft, as she whimpered in the back of her throat. I dug my nails into her waist and dove in further.

Kelly lifted her hips off the couch and moaned.

I continued to drive her crazy by dragging my tongue back and forth. Her chest was heaving, and she was covered in sweat, and I had her completely at my mercy. She kept bucking against me, but I wouldn't give her what she wanted. Eventually, when Liam shifted and came all over the coffee table, Kelly turned her full attention to me.

Smirking, I lifted her legs over my shoulders and thrust into her.

Kelly cried out and raked her fingers over my back.

I buried myself further and began to move with a single-minded purpose. Kelly writhed and spasmed under me. I pinned her arms at her sides and looked into her eyes. She held my gaze as the force of her orgasm ripped through her, leaving her panting and breathless. I gave a few more quick thrusts and spilled into her, heaving a shaky breath as I did.

When I was done, I buried my face in her neck, and she stroked my back.

Hot damn.

I couldn't wait to see what other boundaries she wanted me to test.

Chapter 11

Frank

By Frank Callahan

I fished my phone out of my pocket and peered at the number flashing across the screen. When it rang a second time, I rolled my eyes and shoved it back into my pocket. Then I signaled the bartender for another drink and ignored the vibrating coming from my pantleg.

Denise didn't know how to take a hint.

She was a good fuck, and a part of me loved how hard she could take it, and how much she usually begged for me, but another part of me needed a little variety. Having a big dick had its perks, especially when it turned women into whiny little sluts who would let me get away with anything, but I was getting tired of the same old routine.

As a thirty-eight-year-old black man, I needed something different.

Something spicier.

As soon as the thought left my mind, the door to the bar opened, and a woman with red hair and white skin walked in, wearing jeans that hugged her ample thighs, and a shirt that hugged her body in all of the right ways. Her green eyes scanned the bar, and she pursed her lips. I eyed her over the rim of my glass until her eyes found mine, and she straightened her back.

Shortly after, she was making her way toward me, earning her fair share of looks from the other customers, men and women alike. She gave her hips a little extra sway, then stopped to lean over the bar, offering everyone within proximity a generous view of her cleavage. With a smile, she gave the bartender her order and then hopped onto the stool. When she spun around to face me, I was signaling for my third drink.

"Hi."

I twisted to face her. "Hi."

"You're Frank, right? Jenny told me a lot about you."

I raised an eyebrow. "What did she say?"

Her eyes flittered around the bar before she glanced back at me. One corner of her mouth lifted into a smile. "They say all kinds of things about you."

I curled my fingers around the glass. "You're going to have to be more specific."

Especially if she was going to have an entrance like that.

She held her hand out and showed off a row of pearly white teeth. "I'm Carla."

I stared at her hand for a few seconds before shaking it. "Nice to meet you."

Carla withdrew her hand and smiled at the bald bartender setting down her drink. "So, Frank, you ever think about changing things up?"

I took a long sip of my whiskey. "Excuse me?"

"Well, I've heard that you're here often," Carla began, her green eyes moving steadily over my face. "It's like your watering hole or something, but I would've thought a man like you would want to change things up."

I took another sip of my drink. "Do I know you?"

Carla shook her head, wisps of hair escaping from her messy bun and sticking to her face. "No, but after today, you're going to want to know me."

"Is that so?"

Carla leaned forward and placed a hand on my arm. "Absolutely, because unlike those other women you've fucked, I know how to show you a good time."

Her words went straight to my cock, making it twitch. "What makes you think I haven't been having a good time?"

Having women beg for me still got me all hot and bothered.

It made my blood turn molten, and it made me feel invincible, but I couldn't deny that Carla intrigued me. She didn't strike me as the sort of woman who would allow me to debase her or have her completely at my mercy for my pleasure. On the contrary, she looked like the kind of woman who knew exactly what she wanted and wasn't afraid to go after it.

And the look she was giving me was making my blood boil.

Carla ran her hand up my arm and paused at my shoulders. "Because I can show you a *much* better time, and by the look on your face, seems that you're already interested."

"What if I am?"

Carla removed her arm and reached for her drink. "Let's get out of here, and I'll show you exactly what I mean."

With that, she took her wallet out of her pocket and took out a few bills. She gave me a pointed look on her way past. I hesitated for a brief second before downing the rest of my drink. Then I stumbled after her, my curiosity getting the better of me. We hadn't even kissed yet, and she already had me by the balls.

My pulse skittered as I caught up to her on the street, but she didn't even acknowledge me.

Carla glanced down both sides of the street before crossing. I matched my pace to hers and brushed my hand against hers. Her lips lifted into a half smile as we walked past rows and rows of buildings. A few blocks away she stopped and reached into her pocket. After punching in a code and using the key to unlock the door, she led me into a brown and red apartment building.

She waited for the elevator doors to ping shut before she twisted to face me. "Keep your hands at your sides."

"What?"

Carla took a step closer, the scent of her flowery perfume washing over me. "Don't argue with me. Just do as I say."

I nodded, slowly.

Carla brushed her lips against mine and waited.

When I didn't react, she wrapped her arms around my neck and pulled me down. Her lips were full and hungry. Carla nipped on my lower lip, and when my mouth parted, her tongue darted in. She rubbed herself against me, and I groaned. Then I pushed her against the wall and took hold of her arms.

Immediately, Carla stopped kissing me and pushed me off.

"If this is going to work, you're going to have to do what I say," Carla said breathlessly. "Am I making myself clear?"

"I can't have a little bit of fun?"

Carla leaned forward, her hot breath washing over my face. "Trust me. You're going to like it a lot better this way."

I hesitated and then nodded.

She knew how to work a man, I'd give her that.

When the elevator doors swung open, she motioned to me, and I followed her down a carpeted hallway. At the end of the hallway, she took her keys out of her pocket and looked up at me.

"I want you to touch me while I get the door open. Don't stop until I tell you to."

My blood was pounding in my ears now as I stood behind her. She went through her keys slowly while I rubbed my hands up and down her arms. She shivered, and I resisted the urge to press a kiss to the back of her neck. Then she leaned into my touch, and I rubbed my growing erection against her. Carla made a low noise in the back of her throat, and I pinned her upper arms on either side of her, slowing down her attempt at unlocking the door. But neither one of us was complaining.

I was tempted to fuck her out there in the hallway, regardless of what the neighbors thought.

At least it would give them something to talk about for a few weeks.

Judging by Carla's reaction, I knew she wouldn't mind.

She wanted to call the shots, but I was testing her control, and I wondered how long it would take me to wear her out. Already, I saw myself dragging her back into the elevator, pulling her jeans down, and ramming myself into her. I saw the elevator go up and down while I thrust in and out of her at a steady pace.

Carla was a screamer.

Everyone in her building would know before the day was over.

Before I could do anything else, Carla pushed the door open, and I lost my balance. She whipped around to face me, her face giving nothing away. "Go sit on the couch."

I smirked and wandered into the spacious apartment.

Carla flicked a lamp on, illuminating a brown leather couch set overlooking a fireplace with a mantle and a TV mounted to the wall. Without looking back at her, I peeled off my clothes, taking my sweet time with it in case she was watching. Then I sat down on the couch and draped my arm over the back. When I glanced over my shoulders, she was in the kitchen rummaging through the drawers. She came back out with two glasses and a wine bottle.

"Touch yourself while I strip," Clara instructed in a clear voice. "Do not approach me yet."

She set the glasses and bottle down.

Slowly, she raised her arms over her head and pulled her shirt up, revealing smooth and tanned skin, and a white bra with a lacy black trim in the center. Her chest heaved as her fingers went to the button on her jeans. With a pop, the button came undone, and she spun around to give me a generous view of her round and tight ass.

It bounced as she pushed her jeans down, revealing a matching white thong.

I sat up straighter and stroked myself more intently.

I wanted her on her knees as my dick slid in and out of her mouth. Then I wanted her on all fours, her tits bouncing up and down while I rammed into her from behind. Carla twisted to face me and placed a hand on her hips. Wordlessly, she began to run her hands along her body, and I swallowed.

Holy fuck.

This was the hottest thing I had ever experienced.

She touched herself with purpose like she was trying to tease a reaction. I imagined my hands on her body, ravaging every inch of exposed skin. If it were me, she'd be pressed up against a wall with my hands between her legs, driving her closer and closer to the edge of oblivion. It took every ounce of self-control I had not to get up and crush her to me. And it took even more restraint when she spread her legs apart, and her hand darted underneath her panties.

My breath hitched in my throat. "Why don't I help you?"

"You're already helping me," Carla said, in a thick voice. "You're going to watch until I tell you to, and you're going to like it."

Holy shit.

"I'm not like the other women you've fucked, Frank," Carla continued in the same breathy tone of voice. "In my house, I make the rules, and you're going to obey. You're going to do everything I say and surrender to me completely."

I cleared my throat. "And if I don't?"

Carla stopped touching herself and nodded in the direction of the door. "Then you can leave. I don't negotiate, and I don't compromise."

It was her way or the hard way.

Jesus.

My cock hardened further.

When I didn't leave or get up, Carla smiled and began to touch herself again. She unhooked her bra to let her breasts spill forward. Then she rolled her nipples between her fingers. Once she was done, she hooked her fingers under her panties and pulled them down. Her pussy was already glistening, and I could tell how wet she was even from where I stood.

Goddamn.

How much longer was she going to torture me like this?

"Get up," Carla instructed. "Keep touching yourself as you walk into the bedroom."

I stroked myself furiously and followed her down the dimly lit hallway. She pushed a door open and motioned inside. On my way past, she pressed herself against me but remained still. Her pussy was inches away from my cock, and I twitched with the desire to break her rules. Given how close we were standing, I knew she wouldn't stop me.

Her eyes were daring me to defy her, to break her rules.

But I was too eager to please her.

I curled my free hand into a fist and brushed past her into the room. Carla flicked another lamp on and pointed to the bed. "Climb on the bed and hold your hands out on either side of you."

The bed dipped and creaked as I did what I was told.

My stiff hard-on only grew as Carla bent over the nightstand and opened a drawer. She took out two pairs of handcuffs and climbed onto the bed. She was straddling me as she secured them, and my hips twitched in response to her proximity. Once she secured the handcuffs on either side of the headboard, Carla pressed hot, open-mouthed kisses down my chest and stopped when she reached my happy trail.

She wriggled against me, and I groaned.

"Fuck. You're driving me crazy."

"We're just getting started," Carla said, in a whisper-soft voice. "Tonight, you're all mine, Frank. You're going to do exactly what I tell you to do. Then, and only then, will I fuck the shit out of you."

I pressed my lips together and didn't say anything.

"Do you understand me?" Her lips were inches from mine. "I want to hear you say it."

I swallowed. "I understand."

She gripped the back of my neck and kissed me; hard. Her hand stayed on the back of my neck while the other traced a path down my chest and stopped at my cock. Abruptly, she slid off of me and started to stroke my balls. We were still kissing while she touched me, running her fingers up and down my shaft torturously, each move designed to make me weaker.

To leave me completely and totally at her mercy.

She stroked my balls a little longer, then suddenly, she stopped kissing me. "Good. I can feel how much you want me. You want me to fuck you, don't you?"

"Yes."

"But you like it that I'm torturing you first. You like that you're the one who is tied up for a change."

I blew out a breath. "Yes."

"You're my slave, Frank," Carla told me, pausing so she was sitting on the edge of the bed, her legs stretched out on either side of her. She ran a hand down the front of her chest and down until she reached her center. She used two fingers to spread her lips open and teased the sensitive bundle of nerves there.

Sweat broke out across my forehead and back.

"Do you want to be the one doing this?" Her fingers were darting in and out of her cunt while her breathing changed. She arched her back and moaned. "You want to finger fuck me, Frank, don't you?"

"I do."

"How badly?"

"I want to rip this headboard apart, so I can crawl over there and show you just what you're missing out on. I want to bury my tongue inside that throbbing wet pussy of yours and have you screaming my name."

Carla moaned even louder. "Good. What else?"

"I want to fuck you on every available surface in this house until we both drop from exhaustion."

Carla stopped touching herself and crawled over me. She kept moving until she reached my face. "I'm going to tie you to the bed now, Frank, and then I'm going to sit on your face."

I held myself still as she undid the handcuffs and secured them on either side of the bed. As soon as she did, she lowered herself onto my face and braced herself against the headboard. My tongue immediately darted out, and I licked her swollen pussy lips eagerly. She was drenched already, her juices a mixture of sweet and sour that made me growl.

I squeezed my eyes shut and enjoyed the taste of her.

She liked being devoured like she was some kind of feast.

But she still liked maintaining control which was why she rocked back and forth against my face, her breathing growing heavier and heavier. I wanted to grip her hips and push my tongue in further. I wanted to pin her arms over her head and pinch her nipples.

Fuck me.

How did she have this much power over me?

I swiped my tongue back and forth, alternating between blowing hot air into her center and teasing her. She stopped rocking back and forth and instead bounced up and down. I caught a brief glimpse of her bare tits, begging to be ravished, and I grew harder. Carla twisted an arm over her head and stroked me.

"Men like you were made to serve women like me," Carla said, in a deep and throaty voice. "And you're going to keep serving me until I say we're done."

I sucked harder on her clit. "Fuck."

Carla continued to stroke me, alternating between squeezing my dick and grazing it with her fingers. Eventually, I started to growl like an animal, the sound drowning out everything else, including my own pounding heart. Carla's orgasm ripped through her, leaving her writhing and shaking with pleasure. She called out my name as she rolled off of me and sank onto the mattress. I was tugging on my restraints now, my breathing coming out in short puffs.

Carla propped herself up on her elbows. "What? What do you want, Frank?"

"I want to fuck you." I breathed, molten hot desire racing through me. "I want to fuck you good, like you deserve to be. Like the Queen you are."

Carla climbed on top of me and lowered her head to kiss me. "Now's your chance, Frank. Show me why I shouldn't just walk away and leave you tied up."

Before I knew what was happening, she undid my restraints.

I wasted no time in digging my nails into her hips and thrusting upward. Then I took one nipple between my teeth and tugged. When I moved to the other one, Carla was bouncing up and down against me, and I was trying to match her pace.

We moved with frenzied and animal-like energy.

I sank my teeth into her neck and exploded, the entire body shaking underneath me. I spilled into her and pressed her heaving body to mine. Her orgasm ripped through her, leaving her breathless and panting. Once we were done, she pushed me back and climbed off of me, not bothering to give me a glance back as she left the room with a satisfied sigh.

Conclusion

Thanks so much, friends, for spending this time with me. I'm endlessly grateful that you have chosen one of my books.

If you enjoyed it, please leave a review! It only takes a second, and reviews really help my books reach a broader audience.

Incidentally, if this particle kind of book is... your thing... I think you'd like another one of my books, "Erotic Short Stories for Women Written by Men," which you can find as an ebook, a paperback, or an audiobook.

Be well, dear friends! See you next time.

With love and admiration,

Rayna